"Yusuf?" His breath ghosted across **my cheek.**

"Yeah, Owen?"

"Can you look at me?" With one hand palming my cheek, he used the other to tip my chin back.

Reluctantly I blinked my eyes open.

The quick, easy smile I'd found so fascinating the first night I met him was missing. It had been replaced with something gentler, something more serious.

"I'd like to kiss you. Will you let me?"

Oh man. My heart throbbed, deep and almost sickeningly.

Owen. Owen wanted to kiss me. Kiss *me*. He hadn't asked the night before, which meant this was different somehow. More important, maybe. At least it felt that way.

I sucked in a breath. Licked my lips. Stared into those wide glowing amber eyes.

I wanted to say *yes* and *please* and *okay* and *right now*. But try as I might, the words wouldn't come. So I did the only thing I could do. I nodded.

WELCOME TO

DREAMSPUN BEYOND

Dear Reader,

Everyone knows love brings a touch of magic to your life. And the presence of paranormal thrills can make a romance that much more exciting. Dreamspun Beyond selections tell stories of love featuring your favorite shifters, vampires, wizards, and more falling in love amid paranormal twists. Stories that make your breath catch and your imagination soar.

In the pages of these imaginative love stories, readers can escape to a contemporary world flavored with a touch of the paranormal where love conquers all despite challenges, the thrill of a first kiss sweeps you away, and your heart pounds at the sight of the one you love. When you put it all together, you discover romance in its truest form, no matter what world you come from.

Love sees no difference.

Elizabeth North

Executive Director
Dreamspinner Press

j. leigh bailey

The Night Owl and the Insomniac

Published by

Published by
DREAMSPINNER PRESS

5032 Capital Circle SW, Suite 2, PMB# 279,
Tallahassee, FL 32305-7886 USA
www.dreamspinnerpress.com

The Night Owl and the Insomniac
© 2018 j. leigh bailey.

Cover Art
© 2018 Aaron Anderson.
aaronbydesign55@gmail.com
Cover content is for illustrative purposes only and any person depicted
on the cover is a model.

Mass Market Paperback ISBN: 978-1-64108-049-1
Digital ISBN: 978-1-64080-462-3
Library of Congress Control Number: 2018930551
Mass Market Paperback published July 2018
v. 1.0

Printed in the United States of America
∞
This paper meets the requirements of
ANSI/NISO Z39.48-1992 (Permanence of Paper).

J. LEIGH BAILEY is an office drone by day and romance author by night. She can usually be found with her nose in a book or pressed up against her computer monitor. A book-a-day reading habit sometimes gets in the way of... well, everything... but some habits aren't worth breaking. She's been reading romance novels since she was ten years old. The last twenty years or so have not changed her voracious appetite for stories of romance, relationships, and achieving that vitally important Happily Ever After. She's a firm believer that everyone, no matter their gender, age, sexual orientation, or paranormal affiliation, deserves a happy ending.

She wrote her first story at seven which was, unbeknownst to her at the time, a charming piece of fan fiction in which Superman battled (and defeated, of course) the nefarious X Luther. (She was quite put out to be told later that the character's name was supposed to be Lex.) Her second masterpiece should have been a bestseller, but the action-packed tale of rescuing her little brother from an alligator attack in the marshes of Florida collected dust for years under the bed instead of gaining critical acclaim.

Now she writes about boys traversing the crazy world of love, relationships, and acceptance. Find out more at www.jleighbailey.net or email her at j.leigh. bailey@gmail.com.

By j. leigh bailey

DREAMSPUN BEYOND
#3 – Stalking Buffalo Bill
#13 – Chasing Thunderbird
#23 – The Night Owl and the Insomniac

Published by **DREAMSPINNER PRESS**
www.dreamspinnerpress.com

This book is dedicated to public libraries everywhere.
Without the resources, availability,
and support of public libraries and their staff,
authors like me would be lost!

Chapter One

A GHOST roamed the corridors of Matthison Hall every night.

Okay, maybe I wasn't a ghost, but I sure as hell wasn't living. Not in any real sense. I was a shell of a human, lacking vitality. Lacking personality. Lacking... everything. I'd honestly thought escaping the sterile, nearly clinical existence of my parents' house—not to mention their well-intentioned but completely overwhelming smothering—would change me. Not make me healthy, not that. I'd long given up any hope for medical science to advance enough to diagnose my encyclopedic collection of symptoms, let alone cure me.

I'd hoped going to college—living on my own, doing something normal for once in my miserable life—would somehow actually make me normal. Here at Cody

College I wouldn't be surrounded, monitored, coddled. I wouldn't be pricked, prodded, and tested on a daily— sometimes hourly—basis. There would be no more experimental treatments, no more carefully designed diet plans. I was twenty-one for crying out loud. It was time to live my life on my terms, even if those terms went against medical and parental advice.

By God, if I wanted to eat donuts and pizza at three in the morning, then that was exactly what I'd do.

That particular stride toward independence ended up being a disappointment. Turned out pizza gave me heartburn and donuts made me queasy.

Such was my life.

Instead of celebrating my junk food rebellion, 3:00 a.m. found me drifting through the halls for the tenth night in a row.

Freaking insomnia.

It was bad enough I couldn't easily fall asleep, but the jittery restlessness that came with it made it impossible to even sit still. So instead of going stir-crazy, trapped in the painted cinder block walls of my dorm room, I prowled the residence hall with little faith I'd eventually tire and pass out.

The worst part was, other than the insomnia, I felt better than I had in years. Maybe it was the fresh mountain air, but the debilitating headaches I'd suffered from for as long as I could remember had become less frequent. My body temperature always ran a little high, but there'd been no dangerous fever spikes in the last two weeks. If it wasn't for the twitchy restlessness and the onset of insomnia, I'd have thought I'd finally found an effective therapy.

I pushed into the main lobby, starting to count. It was exactly ninety-seven steps from the entrance of the south wing to the entrance of the north wing. I didn't pay much attention to my surroundings, as I'd made this same trek through the building every night for almost two weeks. Either my physical exhaustion had caused my vision to blur, or a new and less-than-exciting symptom had joined the Medical Mystery Tour that was my life. Or it might have been complacency or obliviousness. Whatever it was, one moment I skirted the bank of student mailboxes on my left, the next I lay sprawling on my back staring up at the boring beige ceiling tiles.

The squeak of rubber on marble told me I wasn't alone. "Holy shit. Dude, are you okay?"

I closed my eyes. I wasn't hurt. In fact, my landing had been relatively smooth, rather like a runner sliding into home on a Slip 'N Slide covered in Jell-O. Speaking of Slip 'N Slide, water seeped through my flannel pajama bottoms. Ick. I planted my hands next to my torso and braced myself to lever off the floor. My right hand landed in a puddle, and I slipped back and found myself reexamining the generic ceiling tiles. Nope. The view hadn't improved.

"What happened? Didn't you see the sign?" The voice, a surprisingly deep voice, wrapped around me like campfire smoke at midnight, reminding me of the single camping trip my dad had taken me on back before I'd gotten sick. The body accompanying the voice dropped next to me. "Careful," the guy said, pressing a hand into my chest as I tried to sit up again. "We should make sure you're okay before you move."

I held my breath at the warmth building at the point of contact between his skin and mine. The thin cotton of my shirt wasn't much of a barrier between us.

It had been so long, years really, since anyone had touched me without the protective layer of vinyl medical gloves. I wanted to press into the touch, to prolong it.

But I couldn't stay here, lounging in… who knew what.

I blinked, trying to clear my vision. It actually helped, which meant my fuzzy focus probably did have more to do with the serious lack of sleep I'd experienced rather than a medical condition. I brought my wet hand near my face and sniffed carefully. I didn't smell anything off-putting, so the puddle was probably water.

"I'm so sorry. I was watering the plants and got a little carried away with this one. I made a bit of a mess, as you can see, and I had to get the mop. The Wet Floor sign was behind the desk, but I had to go to the supply closet to get the mop." His words all rushed together, to the point I wasn't convinced he breathed enough to get them out. Lack of breath clearly didn't stop him, though. "I was only gone for a minute, and I didn't think anyone would be running around at this time of night. At least not on a Tuesday. If it had been a Friday or Saturday, I'd have been more careful."

"I'm fine," I said to cut off the barrage of words. After taking a mental inventory, I admitted I really was okay. No sharp pains or scraped body parts. No aches that hadn't been part of my life 24-7 for the last fifteen-plus years. I brushed aside the hand still pressed to my chest and pushed myself into a sitting position. Part of me really didn't want to break the connection. It felt like the touch, simple as it was, started to fill in the hollow places in my body.

The damn insomnia was making me loopy.

Then I looked up and nearly fell back again.

I'd seen him before. More often than not he manned the front desk of the dormitory during the overnight shift. But none of my midnight wanderings had gotten me close enough to catch those amazing eyes. They were large and round and somehow filled his face in a way reminiscent of an anime character. And they glowed. Well, not glowed, but the irises were the brightest amber—almost yellow—color I'd ever seen on a person. They were, in a word, incredible.

I'd kept my distance whenever I'd seen him at the desk. Not because of anything he'd done or said, but because of me. Because I'd never been good at small talk or chitchat. I didn't do well in social interactions. Like now. Now I was staring at him like a dolt. He started to shift in his squatting position, rocking a bit from side to side, and he rubbed his hands together like he didn't know what to do with them. This. This was what happened when I was left to my own devices with strangers.

I tucked my legs under me so I could stand, making a point to avoid the water. I looked at the soil-flecked moat around the poor drowned plant. Carried away, he'd said. Well, that was one way to put it.

Before I'd gotten any further than a partial crouch, he sprung up, clasped my arm, and dragged me to my feet. "Wow, you're tall. You're sure you're okay? You look pale. I can take you to the urgent care office. They have someone there manning the desk overnight. You know, just in case. My dad's a doctor, and he sometimes gets called in when there's a case the nurse practitioners can't handle. And, oh my God, I keep talking."

I barely caught a word in his excited babble. I was too focused on the feel of his hand wrapped around my forearm. He hadn't let go after I stood solidly on my own two feet. Every second his skin touched mine, the warmth, the life of him seeped into me. He was shorter than me, maybe all of five nine, and stocky with it. Built like a wrestler, solid and broad, but with no extra fat. Aside from his extraordinary eyes, he was kind of average. Average blondish hair, skin a shade somewhere between pale and tan with a handful of freckles scattered here and there.

I probably stared at him too long, silent and awkward, making it even more uncomfortable.

"I'm Owen, by the way. Owen Weyer." When I still didn't say anything—or pull my arm free—he cocked his head to the side. "This is where you tell me your name."

I licked my lips. Right. Conversation. I could do this. "Yusuf." I cleared my throat. "Um, but you can call me Joey." What in the world had prompted me to tell him *Yusuf*? I almost always introduced myself as Joey.

He flashed a smile nearly as wide and bright as his eyes. "Yusuf. I like it. But why Joey?"

I finally remembered to disengage my arm. "Yusuf. It's, ah, like Joseph, but in Persian?" My voice cracked on the last word, turning what should have been a statement of fact into a query.

He seemed to accept this without question. It was a nice change. Every time I met someone new, a new specialist or new nurse, whoever, I almost always ended up getting questions about my name and therefore my heritage. And even those who'd heard of the Persian Empire because they'd read a book or attended a world history class at some point had trouble reconciling my pasty skin tone and hazel eyes with Iran. Apparently they assumed Iranian meant swarthy skin, black eyes, white robes and a kaffiyeh. Which was another reason why my parents, my very Caucasian father and Iranian-born mother, had started introducing me as Joey rather than Yusuf when I was young.

I pulled my attention back to Owen. I'd gotten so used to my own thoughts over the years, it was sometimes too easy to get lost in my head, to the point of forgetting there were things actually going on around me. A direct result, I was sure, of being quarantined—though my parents would probably call it *protected*—from the real world.

"Well, Yusuf, I have to admit I've been wondering about you." The emphasis he'd given it told me the use of my full name had been deliberate.

I liked the way it sounded coming from his mouth; he'd captured the soft, almost slurring *J*-like sound of the first syllable perfectly.

I didn't correct him; I didn't insist he call me Joey, though I'd gone by Joey for as long as I could remember. Even my parents called me Joey. Maybe claiming Yusuf would be one more step in claiming an identity of my own, separate from the sick kid with the overprotective parents.

"Wondering about me?" And look at that. Me actually participating in a dialogue. Maybe I wasn't the most engaging conversationalist, but I hadn't been irredeemably rude. At least, not yet.

"Sure. Like, I've got questions. Lots of questions."

"Questions?" I repeated. Nope, I really, really wasn't going to win any awards in repartee.

"Yeah. You know. Where'd you come from? Why do you wander the building every night? You seem older than the guys who usually live in the dorms, so why are you here? Do you play chess? How about cribbage? You know, questions."

I blinked at him. Questions indeed. I grabbed on to the one question I could answer easily and honestly, without needing to unload my entire pathetic history on him. "I play chess."

"Really? You any good?"

I shrugged. "Depends on how you define 'good.' I've only played online. Do pretty well in intermediate level. Advanced level is hit-or-miss."

The guy—Owen—tilted his head to the front desk. "Want to play? Unless you'd rather spend the night pacing the halls like you've done every other night I've seen you since the summer semester started."

My thoughts screeched to a halt while my brain attempted to make sense of this. An invitation? And he'd noticed me? Something fluttered in my chest, and I didn't think it was arrhythmia.

I had to think about it—balancing the pros and cons of awkwardly interacting with another human in real life. Pros: a way to keep my brain engaged on something other than how totally fish-out-of-water I felt; honest to goodness interpersonal interaction with someone close to my own age; those extraordinary amber eyes. Cons: nearly debilitating social anxiety; complete lack of experience interacting with people my own age—I'd probably say or do something completely wrong; the jittery, coming-out-of-my-skin sensation coursing over every inch of my body.

In the end, the eyes decided it.

"Yeah. Sure. Let's play chess."

WE settled in at the dorm's front desk, which was basically a long counter separating the back office from the lobby. Owen had hauled a tall stool from behind the desk around to the lobby side for me. I wasn't allowed behind the barrier, he explained, because I wasn't an authorized employee. Since the counter was the perfect surface for the chessboard, I saw no problem with the arrangement. He grabbed the chess box from a stack of dilapidated board games, and we divvied up the white and black plastic pieces.

You can learn a lot about a guy by the way he plays chess. Or, at least that's what I'd decided during my online games. Some people were slow and methodical, stretching a game out for hours, sometimes days. I imagined them agonizing over every move, running scenarios, balancing costs and benefits of any given move. Some people played in a sporadic, slapdash way that made me wonder if they lived their lives in such chaos. Some people played as though they were reading a text on chess maneuvers, very by-the-book, even when their opponent didn't play by the same manual.

Owen, he was deceptive. Instead of studying the board, he barely glanced at it before moving one of his pieces. It took me way too long to figure out his moves weren't random. Mostly because I found him distracting. Very, very distracting.

I liked his smile. And he smiled a lot. His smile was just like him, full of life and energy, rejuvenating. Sitting this close to him felt like I was basking in the sun after months in the dark. It was intoxicating and a little scary.

And he talked. A lot.

"I like the night shifts," he was saying while I planned my next move. I had a bit of a conundrum. I couldn't decide whether to push my attack further or shore up my defenses. Somehow, while he'd been giving me recommendations for which professors to avoid next semester, he'd maneuvered his chess army into a subtly threatening position. And because of his casual approach to strategy, I couldn't tell if it was deliberate aggression or a fluke of placement.

"It's a total stereotype, I know, but I've always been a bit of a night owl," he continued, reaching below into a red backpack behind him. He plopped a ziplocked bag of beef jerky onto the countertop while I tried to figure out how liking the night shift was a stereotype. "Help yourself." He motioned to the bag.

I hesitated. The sight of the dried meat and the spicy scent had my mouth watering, but I didn't recognize the brand. I had to avoid foods with too much sodium nitrate, and jerky, depending on the supplier, could be chock-full of it. Just one of many things on the list of possible health triggers I needed to avoid.

Sure, I could have asked to see the bag, to scrutinize the nutritional information on the packaging, but I didn't want to draw attention to my differences. "I'm good, thanks." The whole thing screamed of weakness, so I channeled my self-disgust into my game strategy. Screw defense. I was going on the offense. I moved my knight.

His lips twitched, and he hopped a pawn to the next square. He made a little *boop* sound as the white plastic settled onto its new home. Seriously. He had little sound effects to go with the pieces. Knights zipped, rooks whooshed, pawns booped. It should have been ridiculous. But no, it was charming.

He popped a bit of jerky into his mouth, leaning back on his stool. "There's something so cool about the night, you know? On the surface it's quiet and peaceful and dark. But underneath it all, there's so much going on. Nocturnal predators, nocturnal prey, a constant battle of cat and mouse. We may not see it, but nighttime isn't always quiet and peaceful and dark."

As if to highlight his point, the lobby doors burst open in an avalanche of stumbling men. They laughed, voices echoing in the open space of the lobby. They made enough noise for a dozen people, but a quick glance told me there were only four of them. They stumbled up the counter, two lining up on either side of me. The scent of booze nearly overwhelmed me, and they stood closer to me than I was normally comfortable with.

"Hey, O, my man," one of the guys said with a slur while he offered his hand for a fist bump.

"Mitch. Don't tell me—"

Mitch, a husky-looking guy with a patchy attempt at a beard and a baseball cap, leaned on the counter. "C'mon, Owen. It's not my fault. Well, okay, it is my fault. But I can explain."

Owen leaned on his elbows, clearly trying—and failing—to look disappointed. The way he kept biting back a grin told me the whole thing was for show. "You know I'm not supposed to keep letting you into your room."

"Dude, I know. And I was totally going to remember to bring my key. But, well, I screwed up."

Owen rolled his eyes. "Seriously, Mitch. Next time you'll have to face MacKenzie."

All of them, even Owen, shuddered.

"MacKenzie?" I asked before I thought better of it.

Five heads turned to look at me. I wilted a little at the scrutiny.

"The RA," the drunken guy to my right said.

I'd met the RA when I moved in. He seemed like a decent guy, not someone I would have expected to garner this kind of reaction.

Owen must have seen it on my face. "He's a good guy, and a good RA, but he's a stickler for the rules. If he knew these guys were drinking, he'd have to report them. They're underage."

The guy next to me was the only one of the four who actually looked underage. Maybe due to the lack of facial hair the others seemed to be sporting. He leaned closer to me. I leaned back. I tried to be subtle about it since he wasn't threatening me, just encroaching on my personal space.

"I don't know you, do I?"

"Um, I don't think so."

His exaggerated nod was probably due to his blood alcohol content. "Cool. Who are you?"

"Joey?" I cursed inwardly as my answer came out in a question.

"You weren't here last year, were you?"

Now the other three drunks were leaning in.

"No. I started with the summer term."

"I didn't know you could do that," Mitch said.

"It's not common, I guess."

"You look a little old to be a freshman."

"Oh, well, I'm not. Technically I'm a second-semester sophomore. I took a lot of online classes for some of my gen ed requirements." I hunched in on myself a bit. That was more words than I'd said out loud in weeks.

Mitch peered around his buddy at me. "Hey, are you old enough to buy beer? If we brought you cash—"

"Okay, guys, stop grilling him." Owen came around the counter, a ring of keys dangling from his hand. "Mitch, let's get you to your room." He paused at my stool, then clamped his hand on my shoulder. "I'll be right back. You good?"

"Sure."

When I was alone in the lobby, I released a deep sigh. What a strange night. It was almost dawn, and in the last couple of hours I'd hung out with someone my own age and been interrogated by underage drunks. I glanced down at the chessboard. Narrowing my eyes, I examined the placement of the men. Damn it. In three plays Owen would have my king. Somehow with his laissez-faire playing style, he was going to trounce me. I hadn't seen it coming.

My eyelids drooped, gritty and heavy. For the first time in a while, I thought I might actually be able to sleep.

I tipped my king, forfeiting the game. It was worth the defeat, though, for those first tastes of friendship.

Chapter Two

CODY, Wyoming, was a nice enough town. Sometimes the cowboy theme got a little kitschy, especially in the summer with all the rodeos and reenactments, but the Old West storefronts and the mountains in the distance were a far cry from the concrete-and-brick landscape that made up Chicago. The Windy City was a fine place—top-of-the-line medical facilities, five-star dining, easy access to anything and everything a person could want—but when the time came to break away from my parents' smothering concern, I wanted to get as far away as I could. Not just distance, but attitude and environment. And believe me, after the hustle and bustle of the city, the slower pace and old-world atmosphere was a welcome change.

I adjusted the strap of my messenger bag, wishing I'd brought a baseball cap. I didn't know if it was a result of the higher elevation and the thinner air, but the sun blinded me today. It didn't help when the twitchy, skin-too-tight feeling was worse than it had been, and a mild headache lurked behind my eyes, crouching, waiting to pounce and explode in my brain.

"Hey, Yusuf!" Footsteps pounded behind me, though it took a minute for me to realize the voice was calling for me. It wasn't just the voice—that deep, smoky voice—that told me who rushed behind me. Nobody, not even my mother, called me Yusuf except Owen.

He barreled toward me, halting less than an arm's length away from me. "Whew!" He swiped his hand across his forehead, pushing back his ash-blond bangs along with the slight sheen of sweat on his brow. "I'm glad I caught you. A few of the guys from my afternoon psych class are meeting for lunch. You got plans?"

I stared at him—probably dumbly—for a moment while the words registered. I was twenty-one years old, and no one had ever invited me to lunch before. If that's what it was. Owen didn't actually ask if I wanted to join them. It was more of a statement of his own plans. And, for crap's sake, why was I spinning on this? "Ah... I was on my way to the library."

"Can it wait? Want to come with?"

"Sure." Even as I agreed, my brain screeched at me that I was making a bigger deal out of this than it needed to be. Sure, I was drawn to him in a way I couldn't quite define, so I tried really hard not to make this into more than it was. It was lunch, damn it, not a proposal. A lunch with the guys, even. I'd never done lunch with the guys before.

"Cool!"

Over the last several nighttime wanderings, I'd discovered Owen was a cheerful, easygoing kind of guy. *Affable*, I thought the word was. He was affable. I'd seen him almost every night since our first meeting. Chess matches had become a routine. It had gotten to the point that I didn't wait for the jittery, skin-too-tight feeling to hit before making my way to Matthison Hall's main lobby during Owen's shifts. I finished my homework, took my shower, and headed to the lobby for our now nightly chess games.

Despite the litany of questions he claimed to have at our first meeting, he didn't ask them. He seemed perfectly content to let me sit and play in silence. Not that he was silent, not by a long shot. He told stories, chatted about friends and family, regaled me with tales of campus shenanigans. It was… nice.

It must have been what having a friend was like.

I gripped the strap of my bag as though it were a lifeline as we headed to the Union Center, the all-purpose building that housed the dining hall, the campus bookstore, a small convenience store, and organizational meeting rooms. I hadn't spent much time near the Union Center because, even during the summer semester, it was the one place on campus guaranteed to be full of people. Even after being there a few weeks, I wasn't altogether comfortable in big crowds. I started to relax after a couple of minutes, mostly because it was impossible to stay uptight around Owen. He distracted me with an anecdote about his morning class.

"Then Professor Aaronson throws up her hands and stalks out. Harry and Brendan just stand there, white foam dripping off them like they'd walked through a car wash." Owen gestured from his forehead to his knees before clutching his gut as he dissolved into paroxysms of hilarity.

My lips twitched in an automatic, if unusual for me, smile. "Isn't that your creative writing class? How did they—"

I didn't get the chance to finish my question because a swarm of students, at least ten of them, surrounded us. And despite his use of the word "guys," there were at least four girls in the bunch. Within seconds I was buried in the center of a mass of chatting, laughing, bumping humans. The protective bubble of personal space I usually surrounded myself with—a minimum of two feet—was decimated. Shoulders brushed mine and elbows knocked into me. All light and casual touches, the result of so many people in a limited space, but they set my nerves on edge. Blood rushed in my ears; my breathing sped up. Why were they so close? We were on the sidewalk, for crying out loud; there was no need for everyone to be touching everyone else. It reminded me of a pack of puppies playing together, always needing to be in constant contact with their littermates.

I tripped over a break in the sidewalk while I struggled to get my bearings in such a group. I stumbled forward, but a strong arm—Owen's arm—wrapped around my waist and kept me on my feet. And that touch, that contact, didn't overwhelm me like the others. In fact, it grounded me. The static-filled buzzing in my head receded, and the beat of my heart slowed.

I looked at Owen, and there was a question in his wide amber eyes. *Was I okay*, they asked. Was this okay? And, I realized, it was. After the initial shock of being amalgamated in a boisterous crowd had passed, I actually liked it. The energy of the group, the enthusiasm, was contagious. I smiled at him, letting him know I'd be fine. That I was fine. And in that moment, I really was.

We burst through the dual doors of the Union Center, and we must have looked like a back-to-school advertisement. A dozen smiling, laughing students erupting into the marble corridor.

When we reached the dining hall, our writhing, undulating throng thinned and split as everyone decided which lunch option appealed—the sandwich shop, the salad bar, or the burger joint. It was chaos, the sound and the scents and the people crossing back and forth. It took a moment for my brain to see past the disorder and confusion. I focused my attention on Owen, and like the moment outside, he grounded me.

I stayed close to Owen's side as he made his way to the sandwich shop. He ordered some kind of Italian combo sandwich piled high with onions, hot peppers, and olives. Remembering my heartburn-inducing pizza experiment, I played it safe with a turkey and American cheese sub with no extras. Owen snorted at my selection. "Pretty boring. Is that all you're getting? To be frank, dude, you could use a little more meat on your bones."

I tugged at the hem of the red polo shirt I wore. Yeah, I'd been losing weight lately, not that I had any to spare. But now I probably looked like an eating disorder cautionary tale. Rather than explain about my sensitive stomach, I deflected by sneering at his lunch. "Better than that gastric nightmare. Why don't you throw on the kitchen sink while you're at it?" The minute I said it, I bit my lip. What the hell had gotten into me? I barely ever said more than a couple of words at a time. I certainly didn't snark. Not out loud, at least. And I was still in the process of feeling out this whole friendship thing. I didn't want to offend my first almost-friend.

Rather than act offended, Owen snickered. "Don't knock it until you try it. And the best part is yet to come."

"Yeah?"

He grabbed a bag of potato chips off the display near the register and shook it at me.

"Potato chips are the best part?"

"First, potato chips are always a good choice. But in this instance, the potato chips are going on top of my sandwich. It adds a nice crunchy texture."

I tried to imagine it. It wasn't the worst combination I'd ever heard of. I nodded. "I'd buy that."

We paid for our food and headed to the center of the dining hall where some of Owen's "guys" were pushing two tables together. When the tables and chairs were situated to everyone's satisfaction, Owen dropped into one of the faux-wood-backed seats. Hooking his ankle around one leg, he pulled the chair next to him out and motioned for me to sit.

"Try this."

I blinked at the portion of sandwich that was not my own.

"Huh?" *Great response, Joey.*

"Have a bite and tell me this isn't the best sandwich ever." Owen brought the absurd sandwich combo closer to my mouth.

Not only was he offering me a taste of his sandwich, he was going to feed it to me from his own hand? I blushed. It seemed too intimate, too close. I pulled my head back, and my eyes crossed trying to keep the morsel of food in focus. I caught a whiff of vinaigrette and Italian seasoning. My stomach rumbled; my mouth watered. Then I sneezed. Because of course I did. He jerked back, dropped the sample, and snorted out a laugh. I slapped my hands over my mouth, both in horror and in a knee-jerk cover-your-mouth-when-you-sneeze habit. Then I ducked my head in mortification.

Snickering, Owen wrapped the bits of discarded toppings—casualties in what I feared would be my never-ending battle to not look like an idiot—into a napkin. "Let's try again," he said, grabbing a plastic knife and cutting another slice off his sandwich.

My stomach rumbled again at the sound of plastic cutting through chips and lettuce. Despite that, I held up a hand to stop him. "You don't need to. At this rate you won't have any lunch left. And," I said with an uninspired look at my own sub, "I don't think you'd get the same enjoyment out of turkey and American cheese."

"It's fine. Seriously, you need to see what you're missing." He offered the second sample.

Giving in to the tantalizing scent and an uncomfortable desire to not disappoint Owen, I took it. The flavors exploded in my mouth, and I decided then and there that no matter how bad the heartburn later, I would definitely trust Owen in all things foodie. I groaned at the savory, salty, crispy, and crunchy combination.

"Told you so." With a satisfied smirk, he took a bite.

I looked at my boring sandwich and mourned a little bit. I was hungry enough I could have eaten my sub, Owen's sandwich, and probably every entrée at the table. Lately my appetite had been out of control. I was always starving, and nothing I ate seemed to fill the hole. Too bad so much of what I consumed had been leading to heartburn and stomach cramps. Boring sandwich or not, I didn't waste any time digging in to my less-exciting lunch.

The guy on my right turned to me. "Hi, I'm Jonah." Jonah was a burly guy, probably as tall as I was but bulkier. He had shaggy coffee-colored hair tipped with platinum, as though he'd bleached it at some point and it had mostly grown out.

I swallowed the bite I'd just taken. "Oh, ah, hey. I'm Joey."

"Nice to meetcha." Jonah took a swig from the soda in front of him. "What classes are you taking this summer?" he asked.

"Intro to Wildlife Conservation." There was no lack of good universities in or around Chicago, so I had my choice of schools, but none had a wildlife conservation program like Cody College. My whole life I'd been fascinated by animals and nature. I'd spend hours and hours binging on the Discovery Channel and devouring decades' worth of *National Geographic*s. Cody College, despite being a tiny school in the middle of nowhere, was known for its excellent biology and wildlife programs. The small student population meant my discomfort with crowds was less of an issue too. I really couldn't have picked a better-for-me place to go to school.

One of the four females in the group leaned forward. "Ooh. Is that the one taught by Dr. Coleman?"

"Yeah. I read some of his articles about raptors. I had no idea he'd be so young." Because, seriously, the man didn't look old enough to vote, let alone be as accomplished as he was.

"You should have been here last semester," the girl said. "That's when he started. And Ford! It was a huge scandal."

"Scandal?" Dr. Coleman didn't seem like the type to be part of anything scandalous. Seemed a bit too naïve and geek-like to for anything salacious. I looked at Owen.

"Scandal," he confirmed.

The girl glanced around, then whispered, "He hooked up with his TA."

It was my turn to lean forward. "No. Really? Like, they had an affair?"

She nodded. Owen shook his head. "It wasn't—isn't—like that. They're totally in love. It's almost sickening. As soon as they started dating, they got Ford assigned to a different advisor, both for his thesis work and his TA duties. But it was pretty hot gossip for a while."

"Ford… that's a guy, right? So this Ford and Dr. Coleman are gay?"

"Or bi. I don't know specifically. Is it a problem?" Something in Owen's voice told me it had better not be a problem.

"Not for me," I said honestly. I hadn't had much time to explore my own sexuality in any real way—being hospitalized for the lion's share of one's life made dating and sex difficult—but I was pretty sure I fell somewhere under the LGBTQIA+ spectrum, especially after spending time with Owen.

"Owen's gay," Jonah announced.

I shot a look Owen's way. I'm not sure what the right response would have been, and since it didn't seem appropriate to mention the little thrill shooting through me, evidence of my place under the rainbow umbrella, I went with the very insipid "Um, okay."

Owen reached behind me and smacked Jonah upside the head. "Smooth, dude."

Jonah ducked away. "Hey, just putting it out there. I know you're digging hi—"

Owen reached behind me—again—and smacked Jonah upside the head—again—color blooming across his neck and face.

I was pretty sure there was some kind of subtext there I should have picked up on. But subtext wasn't really my strong suit. Things were quiet, uncomfortably so, for a couple of minutes. Then one of the guys at the other end of the table asked a question about one of the readings they had to do for their psych class.

Chapter Three

I GROANED, curling into the fetal position on my narrow bed. After years of being sick, I was finally dying. And if death wasn't imminent, someone owed me a serious explanation. It had started the day before with mild, if sporadic, discomfort. Stiff joints, sore muscles, and a bone-deep ache that grew with every hour.

Tearing pain ripped through me as I dragged myself from my bed to dig through the plastic tub of random first aid and medical supplies. There had to be something. Even an aspirin. At this point an aspirin would mostly be useless, but anything—anything—would be better than this. My head throbbed, huge and hollow, with every beat of my heart. Pressure built, like someone was blowing up a balloon that was encased in an eggshell. My brain was the balloon, my skull the shell. For a while the outer casing would hold, but eventually the balloon would grow too big and the shell would burst. God, I wanted the shell to burst.

The light in my small room burned my eyes, and I squinted at the adhesive bandages and antibiotic ointment in my first aid kit. Useless. It was all completely useless.

I needed to call 911—

Agony swept through me on a wave of misery. My whole body clenched and my spine bowed. I swore I could hear my bones cracking under the viselike pressure. I choked back a sob as the box of useless medical supplies crashed to the floor.

The narrow white walls pressed in all around me. Overwhelming. Suffocating. It was too much. Too much. Too much.

I scrambled to my feet and grappled with the door handle. Out. I had to get out. Out of this room. Out of this building. Outside. Just… out.

God, I hurt. It felt like someone was tugging on my muscles. Pulling, stretching, dragging. Never in all my years in the hospital, facing one mysterious symptom after another, had I felt anything like this. My body was fighting itself, turning inside out. This had to be what being drawn and quartered felt like.

I didn't know exactly what I was doing or where I was going. Everything around me looked like I was seeing it through green glass, likely a sign the pressure in my head was reaching critical. A small part of me, one that held itself back a bit, one that observed rather than experienced life, wondered if I was having a stroke. Or an aneurysm. The rest of me was driven by pure instinct, a primal drive chanting *outside outside outside*.

I stumbled down the hall to the stairs. The slap of my bare feet on the polished gray concrete bounced off the walls and echoed in the dark chute above me. Everything was so loud. Too loud. My ears rang and vibrated like someone had flicked a tuning fork directly on my eardrum. The stairwell, usually dimly lit, seemed excruciatingly bright. I squinted against the retina-piercing neon-bright beams lasering out the little glass windows in the steel doors.

I somehow descended the two flights of stairs between my room and the ground floor without falling and breaking my neck. I charged past the empty study lounge, my feet carrying me faster and faster to the exit. I needed fresh air. The moon. Green grass.

I burst through the side exit and sucked in a deep breath of fragrant mountain air. And something deep inside eased.

The balloon in my head was still inflating, and my muscles were still being pulled in a dozen directions, but my vision started to clear and I could breathe. And I could think.

I was in trouble. I'd told myself when I escaped from my parents' care that I could and would deal with any of my health problems on my own, but the first time I was confronted with something new, I panicked.

But this wasn't an iron deficiency or some autoimmune reaction. It wasn't fatigue or fever or vomiting.

This was worse. Bigger. All-consuming.

Owen. Owen had said there was an urgent care clinic on campus. I had to find it. Or find Owen.

The wind shifted, and chills racked my body. I broke into a cold sweat, and I realized I wasn't wearing a shirt; only flannel pajama bottoms covered any part of me. I crossed my arms over my chest as an attempt to keep my body warm in the temperate evening air, but also because I felt oddly exposed standing in the dormitory's courtyard.

Owen. I needed to find....

It seemed to take forever, but I finally stumbled my way to the front of Matthison Hall. I pressed my nose against the thick glass, trying to make my uncooperative eyes focus. A silhouette of a man shifted. The shadow morphed, distorted, first tall, then wide, then wobbly along the edges before it snapped back into its solid form. A form taller and thinner than Owen.

Damn it, I needed it to be Owen at the desk tonight. He'd know what to do, who to call.

I stumbled back, catching my heel on the edge of the sidewalk crossing in front of the dormitory. I windmilled my arms, but it felt like I was trying to move them through a rushing tide of water. Gravity grabbed hold of me and dragged me down. I didn't feel the landing, neither the scrape of concrete against my bare feet nor the pitted asphalt beneath my head. Everything—sound, touch, scent—was muffled, like I really was submerged in an ocean's worth of water.

Above me, a platinum nimbus formed around the outer edges of slate-gray clouds. They parted, revealing the full moon in all her opalescent glory. Broad and clear, it dominated the skyscape.

I caught my breath in awe. Never had I seen the moon so big or so clear.

Then I caught my breath for another reason altogether. The balloon in my head finally reached its limit. The shell holding everything—the pressure, the hollowness—shattered, and everything snapped off.

"HOLY shit. Who is that?"

"Is he dead?"

Voices. Unfamiliar voices surrounded me.

I tried to force open my eyes, but they didn't want to move. In fact, my whole body seemed to be stuck. I struggled, trying to break through the paralysis gripping me. No. No. No. I refused to accept that my body would betray me in such a way. Not now. Not after everything else it had already put me through.

"Of course he's not dead."

I knew that voice. Didn't I?

Something warm and firm pressed against my wrist in a way that felt familiar. Routine. I tried to think past the fear gripping me. If I could understand what was happening, I could actually do something about it.

"He's got a pulse," the voice I could almost place said. Pulse. Right. That's what felt so familiar. Someone taking my pulse.

Did that mean I was back in the hospital? No. No, I didn't want to go back. The alarm I'd managed to push away came creeping back. I tried to shake my head, but the effort caused lighting to shoot from my skull to my toes. Shit. Was I broken?

"Careful," the deep voice soothed. "Don't move yet."

"Owen, what happened?" This voice was female and anxious. "There's not blood, is there? You know I can't handle—"

"You know, I don't get it." A male—young, cocky—snorted from somewhere near the anxious girl. "How can you be squeamish? You hunt every month—"

"I'm not squeamish. I just don't like—"

I tuned out the conversation; it wasn't a difficult thing to do with the sound of blood rushing in my head. Besides, the speakers, their words, didn't mean anything to me. I focused instead on the hands—I could feel the broad palms and strong fingers—cupping my face.

Those hands felt very capable as they traced around the back of my head, down my neck, across my shoulders. I wanted to nuzzle into those touches, to increase the pressure of the contact. When the hands moved away, I heard a soft whimpering. In some distant part of my foggy brain, I recognized the sound as having come from me.

"Jesus, Owen, are you seriously copping a feel right now?" Cocky Boy again.

"Don't be an idiot. I'm checking for blood or broken bones."

That was enough to penetrate the fog in my brain. My breathing sped up until I was panting, each abbreviated inhalation doing nothing to bring oxygen to my starving lungs. I felt a tear slip from the corner of my eye.

"Oh, hey. Shhh. It's okay. Relax." Those hands—Owen's hands—were back, brushing away the tear. "You'll be fine."

I had no reason to believe him, but... I did.

"Should we call 911?" Anxious Girl asked, sounding even more anxious.

"No. Human doctors wouldn't know what to do with him."

Human... excuse me? I renewed my efforts to move, to open my eyes, to talk. Maybe I was in a coma? Stuck in my own twisted dreams? Because... human? Since when did we differentiate between human doctors and doctors?

"You mean he's not human?" Cocky Boy.

Stop saying *human*. This had to be a dream. It was last week's pizza at three in the morning that did this. Or the crazy Italian sandwich with potato chips Owen had forced me to try the other day. It had to be. Otherwise my twisted psyche owed me one hell of an explanation.

"Of course not. He's a shifter. Cat of some kind."

"How can you tell?" Anxious Girl.

"*Tapetum lucidum*," Owen explained.

Huh?

Cocky Boy was as confused as I was. "Huh? What does that mean?"

I felt Owen push gently at my left eyelid. My eyes were rolling uncontrollably, as though they were desperately trying to investigate my brainstem from the inside, so I wasn't sure what he was looking for. "Tapetum lucidum," he said, moving to my right eye. "It's the reflective membrane in the eye that causes some animals' eyes to reflect light in the dark. For crying out loud, you should know this. It's one of the easiest ways to identify most shifters."

There was that word again. *Shifter.*

"Fine. So he's got the taciturn lidocaine whosiwhatsit. But if we can't call an ambulance, what should we do? I mean, we can't leave him lying in the middle of the walkway like this. Can we?"

I needed to move. Maybe I was trying to do too much at once. Maybe if I started smaller…. I concentrated on my fingers. If I could move one finger, I could move two. And on and on until I could sit up and demand Owen and his band of misfit coeds stop spouting nonsense.

Owen let out an impatient huff. I could feel the moist puff of his breath against my face. "Of course we're not going to leave him here. It's the full moon. Who knows what would happen to him." I could tell he pulled away from me, and the loss of the connection—the loss of his touch—distracted me from my futile game of anatomical concentration. "I'm going to call my dad, and we're going to take him to the clinic."

Forget the fingers. I changed my focus to my mouth. And my vocal cords. Enough was enough. I needed to tell them to knock it off. It wasn't funny anymore. And I needed to wake up immediately. Clinic meant doctors. Doctors meant tests and medical history forms. It didn't matter to me that earlier I'd been in so much pain I'd have willingly walked miles for an aspirin. I wasn't in pain now, and if I could only get my fucking eyes or mouth to work, I could tell someone so.

Owen murmured in the background, and Anxious Girl and Cocky Boy whispered to each other. I was so absorbed with my own internal dialogue, I didn't have the capacity to worry about what anyone else was saying. Move, damn it. Do something. Anything.

At first I thought it was wishful thinking. The little tingles started at my toes and the tips of my fingers. Little shocks, like synapses firing again. Then a rushing current enveloping me.

"Um, Owen? He's moving." Anxious Girl's voice quavered.

"What—oh, shit!"

Finally. My body was doing… something. Pressure. It went on forever, this inexorable pressure. Building, tightening, straining. Then, for the second time that night, I shattered.

I roared. In pain. In ecstasy. In terror. In relief.

"Holy shit." Cocky Boy's hushed voice quavered. "Is that… is that a lion?"

Chapter Four

IT was like someone shone a spotlight on the grass and walkway in front of Matthison Hall. Every blade of grass, every ant inching along the sidewalk came into clear focus. I could see *everything*. Lines were cleaner, sharper, colors truer than ever before. Shadows didn't fuzz the focus in the least.

I turned toward Owen, Anxious Girl, and Cocky Boy and immediately wished my vision were not suddenly so acute. Their faces were pale, and Owen looked on with wide-eyed shock. Anxious Girl, a slim blonde with a long ponytail, looked ready to faint from horror or panic. I recognized Cocky Boy from lunch the other day. He'd been sitting next to that Jonah dude. He didn't look so cocky now. In fact he stumbled back when I swung my head in his direction, and he tripped on the sidewalk much like I had earlier. He landed on his ass, then crab-walked until his back came up against brick façade of the dormitory.

I took a step toward him, or tried to. My legs didn't seem to know how to follow the directions from my head. Like intent and muscle control no longer worked together. My limbs lost all strength, and I collapsed into a heap on the grass.

Owen lunged forward as if to help me out, then jerked back, apparently thinking better of it.

I shook my head to try to clear it. Which is when I caught a glimpse of a reflection in the glass of the main entrance.

Holy shit. There really was a lion—or something that looked a bit lionish—on campus. It sprawled in the grass like an awkward house cat that had just slipped on polished marble floors.

I tried to push myself up so I could run, get away. Even as I did it, the lion-thing stood from its sprawl.

I hollered.

It yowled.

I sidled to the left.

It matched me, stumbling step for stumbling step.

And that's when I finally understood. I had passed out and was stuck in some kind of demented dreamscape. Either the stress of independence or the trauma of the pain I'd experienced had landed me in this nightmare. I went to pinch myself awake, but the claws at the end of my paw—holy crap, I had paws! And claws!

"Yusuf?" Owen took a cautious step forward, holding his hand out.

"Are you crazy?" Cocky Boy whisper shouted.

The tone grated, but more than that, I didn't like the accusation against Owen. I snarled. I seriously snarled at someone. The sound ripped through the tension, ratcheting up the alarm in the air.

Owen moved back, placing himself in front of Anxious Girl. He gestured behind him, indicating Cocky Boy should back up. "Hey, Gene?" He barely moved his mouth and clearly tried to keep his voice soothing, but the apprehension dulled the effect a bit. "I need you to go to the front desk. There's an emergency locker beneath the counter. The code is 5-5-6-3-2."

"Code?" Cocky Boy asked weakly.

"5-5-6-3-2," Owen repeated. "There's a tranquilizer rifle for emergencies. Bring it and the packet of shifter tranquilizer darts."

"On it."

"You're going to shoot him?" Anxious Girl asked.

Oh hell. He's going to shoot me?

"I'm going to knock him out so he doesn't hurt himself or anyone else."

My fight-or-flight instincts were at war. I wanted to run, to get away from this psychotic situation. Even if it was a hallucination or some kind of coma-induced dream, I knew I didn't want to be here, not like this. But I was too scared to run, and a soul-deep protective instinct had me ready to defend myself against... whatever the hell this was. I paced in a looping figure-eight pattern, wanting to run, unable to leave.

"What's wrong with him?"

Owen shook his head. "I'm not sure. I don't think he knows what's going on."

He had that right. I had no fucking idea what was going on. I had a tail. A fucking tail!

Movement in the reflection caught my attention. Cocky Boy—er, Gene—rushed out carrying some kind of rifle-shaped gun.

That was all it took for the flight combatants to defeat the fighter soldiers in my inner battle. I spun, crouched, and sprang away. It didn't matter that I thought this was some messed-up dream. It didn't matter that I had no idea where I was going. It didn't matter that I didn't know how to survive as some kind of animallike creature. I had to flee, to escape. So I ran.

For about three seconds.

A muffled *pop* sounded, quickly followed by a stinging pinch at my haunch. Then, three strides later, my knees—were they still called knees on a lionlike creature?—buckled. Two seconds later, I was out.

"I CAN'T believe you called Buddy, Dad. Seriously?"

"He's the only local big enough and strong enough to handle a feral lion, Owen."

For the second time that night—was it still night?—I woke to the sound of voices and paralysis holding my body hostage. Or maybe the rest had been a weird dream and I'd open my eyes and find myself in my dorm room, staring at the blank white wall.

Of course if I was in my room, then someone needed to explain why there were people talking. I didn't have a television, and I lived alone, so....

I chuffed, the sound foreign and a little scary. I did not, as a habit, chuff. My breathing sped up, and I struggled to move, to open my eyes. Relief surged through me when my lids cracked. Maybe I wasn't paralyzed after all, just sluggish. I couldn't tell where I was; all my open eyes showed me was a butter-yellow surface, like a wall or a panel. I tried to lift my head to get a better feel for my environment. I gained about half an inch; then I dropped.

There was a scent in the air, something earthy and rich. Like boulders buried in soil and fir trees in the fall. And male, and power, and dominance. And since when did dominance have an odor?

"But Buddy? He's not exactly an enforcer. No offense."

Something released an ululating rumble nearby, and the skin along my neck and spine tingled in warning. So, naturally, I hissed.

Everything—everyone?—around stilled.

"Is he waking up?"

It suddenly clicked for me that Owen was there again. Or was it still? I couldn't quite wrap my head around everything that had happened, or what I had dreamed happened, earlier.

"Stay back!" the other voice—this one older, but with the same deep smokiness Owen's held—commanded.

I snarled. I really didn't like someone talking to Owen that way.

And what was with the weird noises? I didn't even snore, not that I knew of, let alone chuff, hiss, and snarl.

I tried to lift my head again, and this time it worked a little better. I gained enough visibility to recognize I really was facing a wall. Like my dorm, it was painted cinder blocks, but the butter-yellow color told me it wasn't Matthison Hall. The paint wasn't clean or unblemished. In fact, it looked like something had clawed the hell out of it. Actually, it looked like lots of somethings of various kinds had attacked the wall with claws and teeth. Dismay skittered along my spine. This didn't seem like the kind of place I'd be safe hanging out in.

I turned my head and saw bars running vertically from the concrete ceiling to the concrete floor. Yeah, like the scratches in the wall, bars and concrete were bad signs.

And Owen was here? Was he being held in some kind of cell? Because sure as shit, I was in some sort of prison cell.

A little strength had returned, so I used it, and the fierce protectiveness fueling it, to roll over. It took way more effort than it should have for something as simple as a roll. My limbs didn't seem to be in the right place, and my body seemed to be weighed down, but eventually I completed the turn. And immediately wished I hadn't.

In front of the cell bars—and yes, I was absolutely being held in some kind of cell—stood Owen and a man who looked like an older version of my friend. And a monstrous, silver-tipped grizzly bear.

I surged to my feet, adrenaline, and an instinctive need to protect, to dominate, overriding the lingering paralysis in my body.

Owen stepped forward.

The older guy jumped back.

The bear thundered.

I roared.

Holy shit. I *roared*?

For the first time, I looked down at myself and saw not the tall, gangly young man I should have seen. No, instead I was confronted with ruddy black-speckled fur, feline paws the size of hub caps, and a tufted tail.

I stumbled back, landing on my haunches. It hadn't been a hallucination or a nightmare. I really was stuck in the body of a lion. Or something lionlike.

I jerked my head up, looking for Owen. Looking for an explanation.

Sympathy softened his face. "It'll be okay. You're fine, Yusuf." He turned to the older man. "Dad, I really don't think he knew about shifters. He was completely terrified when he shifted."

Dr. Weyer—because if this was Owen's father, that made him the doctor who sometimes worked at the urgent care clinic on campus—shook his head. "It seems unlikely. How old is he? Even in individuals with delayed shifts, the first shift happens before puberty."

"He's at least twenty, but you weren't there, Dad. I've never seen a shift like it. It wasn't instantaneous like it should be. I'm not exaggerating when I say it took almost a minute. At least forty-five seconds."

"Are you sure it wasn't stress of the moment? Time always seems to slow down at—"

I shook my head even as Owen did the same. Even assuming the agony of the moment inflated the timing—and I was 99 percent sure Owen's estimation of forty-five seconds was about forty-five seconds short of reality—it sure as hell hadn't been instantaneous.

"It was painful to watch, Dad. I shouldn't have been able to see enough for it to be painful to watch."

The older Weyer gave in. "Okay. We need him to shift if we're going to figure any of this out."

"At least it looks like he's tracking better now. Definitely less feral."

Dr. Weyer approached the cell, straightening his shoulders. "Yusuf, I need you to change back now. We need to talk."

He had to be kidding me. If I knew how to reverse my sudden occupation of a lionlike thing, didn't he think I'd have done it by now? I really wasn't digging my new appearance. If I'd been in my human skin, I'd have rolled my eyes. Instead I shrugged as best as I could with my new form. Owen chuckled, so I didn't think it conveyed the information I was going for.

"Please, Yusuf. We can't work any of this out until you can talk to us."

Owen rolled his eyes at his father. I was glad it worked for one of us.

"I don't think he knows how."

"Well, he can't stay shifted. If he's as inexperienced as you say, the longer he stays in this form, the more he risks getting stuck that way forever. And truly feral shifters have to be put down before they hurt themselves or someone else."

I cocked my head and whined.

The grizzly, who'd been watching the exchange like a spectator at a volleyball game, rumbled and ducked his head twice in a sharp nodding motion.

"Good idea, Buddy." Owen patted the huge bear on his broad neck as though he were a Labrador rather than an apex predator.

I snarled again, wanting them to share the good idea with the group. I was all for any good idea that would let me ditch the fur and claws. And get me some damn explanations.

"Right. Yusuf, this is something that usually works with toddlers who experience their first shift." Dr. Weyer rubbed his hands together, clearly ready to get down to business. "I want you to watch Buddy. He's going to change back to human. Sometimes, when we are acting primarily on instinct, proximity to another shifter during the change can trigger our own shift."

While I wasn't excited to be on a level with a toddler, any plan, even one hinging on proximity to another shifter, was better than being stuck as a big cat. I jerked my head up and down. Hopefully it came off as leonine and majestic, not uncoordinated. If I had to communicate in animal form, being majestic was the least I could ask for.

The grizzly shook out his fur before ambling closer to the cell I was stuck in. His gaze met mine and held. I stiffened, ruff prickling, and something primal deep inside me recognized the eye contact as a challenge. The bear didn't seem put off by my wary reaction to him. Thankfully there was no posturing or growling. I didn't know what this strange monster inside me would do in any kind of confrontation. Which would kick in, flight or fight?

Then something… miraculous? Astounding? Unbelievable? … happened. The air around the bear wavered, like a heat haze in the summer, and then instead of a bear the size of a small elephant, a man stood. Burly and naked, yes, but he was definitely human. My jaw dropped, and I tried not to think about how dumb I must look.

"Once more, I think," Dr. Weyer said.

The naked man nodded. A second later the shaggy bear stood in front of me.

"Are you ready to try it?"

He had to be kidding. I hadn't seen anything. How was I supposed to emulate something I'd never seen before?

"Just a second." Owen left his place behind the bear/man and hustled forward. "This time," he said, wrapping his hand around one of the metal bars separating us, "while you watch Buddy, try to clear your mind. Relax. And picture your human form."

I released a breath.

Owen kept talking, his voice soothing, hypnotic. "You're tall. Think about your long legs, the curve of calf muscle, the bend of the knee. Imagine your hands. You've got big hands, right? Broad palms, long fingers. Think of the little things that make you human. Things like your belly button and your Adam's apple."

Sensation ghosted along each body part he mentioned, and when he mentioned belly button, I almost laughed. It tickled, and all those sensitive nerves tied into that little knot throbbed. It was then, at the very odd and purely human tug deep inside my gut, that Buddy the bear shifted. It felt like a warm wave of energy swept through the room and along the floor before surging up and around us, pulling me up like a marionette by its strings. One second I was squatting on the floor of a jail cell/animal kennel, the next I stood, shaking, in front of my new friend, his physician father, and a naked man.

I gasped in a breath, as though I'd been at risk of drowning, then immediately collapsed to the cold floor. I was weak and shaking, and I was 90 percent sure I'd be vomiting any minute now.

Owen crouched in front of me. The bars separating us wavered in my vision. Then I realized I was wavering, not the cage. "It gets easier. Next time you—"

I shook my head, a little amazed the gesture was pain-free. "No. Nope. No way. Never doing that again. Not ever."

Owen cocked his head, eyes wide as he searched my face. Maybe trying to see if I was serious? It suddenly dawned on me—Owen was probably a shifter. Everyone in this room turned into an animal. And it hit me again that this was some messed-up shit. I crab-walked backward, putting distance between me and him. The bars of the cell didn't seem like much protection against someone who could change forms at will.

"Yusuf?" Owen carefully adjusted his position until he sat on his ass, legs sprawled out in front of him. It was about as nonthreatening as a person could get. "Relax, okay? Your eyes are glowing, which means you're about ready to shift again."

I squeezed my lids shut, both to hide the glow and to try to wrestle some control back. I started reciting the Persian alphabet in my head, a trick I'd used to calm my nerves before some of the more invasive medical testing I'd faced. I'd only gotten about halfway through the thirty-two characters when I felt sufficiently calm. I opened my eyes.

"Good," Owen murmured. "That's good."

Something moved in the periphery of my vision. I jerked my head around to see Buddy the bear/human slipping on a pair of worn-nearly-white jeans. A few things crossed my mind as I watched this. First, the man went commando. Second, I was bound to have an inferiority complex the rest of my life after seeing the size of his dick. And third, damn it, I was nude too.

No one else seemed concerned that I sat in a naked sprawl. Maybe they saw naked people every day. Which, come to think on it, they probably did. Me, I wasn't so sure how to be blasé about something like public nudity. I pulled my knees up and angled my body to keep the more intimate parts of me covered.

"Any chance I can get something to, ah—" I gestured to my bare chest.

Owen looked startled by my request at first, but after a second he nodded and turned to his father. "You got anything around here?"

Dr. Weyer went to a cabinet on the other side of the room, and I took my first real look at the place Owen had brought me to. Outside the cell, the pale yellow walls were in better condition, cleaner, without strips of paint missing from where any animals—shifters?—had clawed at it. The rest of the room looked like the typical doctor's examining room, but sized for bears. The exam table was big enough to hold Buddy and then some. The scale in one corner looked like something out of a farm vet's office and was wide enough to throw a dance party on. A long counter was built into the wall along one side of the room, though there were no canisters of cotton swabs or boxes of Kleenex breaking up the flat expanse of blue Formica.

Dr. Weyer reached into an industrial-sized locker and pulled out a blue hospital gown. At the sight of the chintzy cotton, my stomach heaved and something tightened around my throat, making it hard to swallow and hard to breathe. I'd seen more than my fair share of those stupid gowns. I couldn't face throwing one on now. I'd rather be naked. Seriously.

Biting his lip, Owen turned to his father. "Hey, Dad? You got any spare clothes around here? He's not here for surgery. Sweats and a T-shirt should be fine."

"We keep some things in the closet in the hall. But given everything that's happened, I think an exam is in order, don't you?"

I swallowed back the bile creeping up my throat.

I knew in an intellectual kind of way that an exam was most definitely in order. I'd turned into a fucking wild animal, after all. A checkup by a doctor was the least I needed. But my intellect couldn't win a fight with the visceral terror and revulsion coursing through me.

"I get it." Owen may have been talking to his father, but his eyes never left me. "But maybe we can make it a little more casual? Maybe a conversation rather than an examination?"

Dr. Weyer's face cleared, and I realized his mind had been half occupied with something else. He narrowed his eyes and really looked at me. His piercing stare made me squirm, wondering what truths he was boring out of my psyche.

"You got this under control, Doc?" the big man who was apparently a part-time bear asked.

"Oh, yes, thank you, Buddy. You were a tremendous help."

Buddy shrugged. "I had the time." He was apparently a man of few words. Since I tended to keep most of my words inside my head, I could appreciate his restraint.

"I'll buzz you out." Dr. Weyer followed the bigger man to the door. He looked over his shoulder at Owen. "I'll bring some clothing. And, Owen?" He waited for Owen to make eye contact. "Keep the cage locked until I'm back."

Chapter Five

"SO, on a scale of one to ten, how freaked-out are you?"

A laugh with only a tinge of hysteria coloring it burst out of me. "Oh well, you know. Maybe a thirty."

Owen grimaced and nodded. "Yeah, I bet."

I wrapped my arms around my knees, making sure I didn't flash my junk at Owen in the process. "What's happening to me?"

"I wish I knew. I take it you weren't aware you were a shifter?"

This time there was more than a tinge of hysteria in my laugh. "I'm not even sure what a shifter is."

He shook his head. "That's... wow, I don't even know what to do with that. I mean, how can you not know?"

"Easy. People who turn into animals don't exist. Shouldn't exist. Whatever. Why in the world would I suspect I was one?"

"It's part of your heritage, of who you are."

"I'm pretty sure I'd have noticed sprouting fur before now."

"Well, yeah, that's what I mean. Usually someone's first shift happens when they're pretty young. I've never heard of anyone changing for the first time when they're in their twenties."

I shrugged. "Just one more way I'm special, I guess."

He didn't seem to know what to say to that, so we sat in awkward silence for a moment. I caught the lingering traces of bear on the air. I licked my lips and voiced one of the dozen or so questions clamoring for attention in my brain. "Uh, why did you bring in the bear? I mean, I assume you're a shifter too, right? Or how else would you know so much about it? Couldn't you or your dad have done the same thing to spur on my change?"

His gaze flicked to his feet before bring coming back to mine. "Well, that was my dad. I mean, yeah, we're shifters—great horned owls, to be specific—but we're too small. There was no telling if your feral half would have recognized our humanity or simply thought we were prey."

If I opened my eyes any wider, they'd probably spill out of their sockets. "So you had to bring in a bear?"

His lips quirked, but he didn't really smile when he answered. "I don't think you realize how big you really were. You're a lion of some kind. Like, three-hundred-plus pounds of pissed-off cat. We needed something just as big, just as strong, nearby in case you woke up violent."

I thought about the reflection I'd seen in Matthison Hall's front windows. "Lion? Are you sure? It didn't look right for that."

"Some kind of lion. The body shape was right, even if the mane was a little shorter than what I'd have thought. Maybe a juvenile lion? Maybe you're not quite fully grown or formed?"

Before I could say anything, the doctor was back, a stack of folded clothes in his hands. He rolled them and passed them through the bars to me. The action reminded me that I was actually behind bars, something I'd been trying not to notice. Remnants of the too-tight feeling that led me to pace the halls at night instead of sleep skittered along my skin, and I broke into goose bumps.

I wrapped my arms around myself, anchoring each elbow with the opposite hand. "Any chance you'll let me out of here?" I jerked my chin to the gate of the cell and the monster steel lock keeping me in.

Dr. Weyer looked askance at his son, then at me. "I think we should—"

"Here's the thing. Being locked in, trapped, is kind of freaking me out." The walls of the cell felt like they were closing in on me even as I said the words.

"Is the tranq gun loaded?" Dr. Weyer asked Owen.

"Yeah, but—"

"Keep it handy." Owen's dad pushed the last of the clothes—a blue T-shirt—through the bars, then reached into his pocket and retrieved a ring with a dozen keys.

I snatched the shirt and the sweatpants that preceded them and tugged them on, even while the doctor took his time inserting the key. I got it. I really did. He wanted to protect himself and his child. My dad would have done the same thing. To try to ease his mind, I stood toward the back of the built-in cage and let my arms dangle nonthreateningly at my sides. I took a minute to try to calm my brain, to slow my breathing.

Dr. Weyer swung the door open and stood aside, careful to keep a safe distance between us as I passed by him. When it was clear I wasn't going to rush him or Owen, he let out a breath of his own.

I searched for pockets to shove my hands into, but the generic sweats, which were about four inches too short for me, didn't have any, so I crossed my arms again. It might be a closed-off look, but I needed to hide my trembling hands. "So… um, how long was I out of it?" There were no clocks I could see in this supersized exam room. Of course, even if I knew what time it was now, I didn't really know what time I'd stumbled out of my room.

"You were only knocked out"—Owen winced when he said it, as I remembered it had been he who shot me with the tranquilizer gun to begin with—"for about twenty minutes."

"A shifter's body metabolizes quickly, so it didn't take long for the effects of the tranquilizer to wear off."

Shifter. There was that word again. "Are you going to be able to explain any of this to me?"

"Sure. We'll talk while I examine you. I don't like those circles under your eyes, and you look about thirty pounds underweight for your height."

As if agreeing I needed to eat more, my stomach rumbled loudly enough we all heard it.

"I think we'd better feed you. Owen, there are some protein bars in the clinic's breakroom upstairs. Grab some, will you? In fact, bring the whole box."

I didn't want Owen to leave, which was stupid. His father likely had all the answers I needed.

"I'll be quick," Owen said, as though he'd caught my hesitancy.

I nodded, relieved.

After Owen had darted out of the room, clearly intent on fulfilling his promise to be quick, Dr. Weyer gestured to the oversized examination table. I hitched myself up onto it, cringing at the shifting sound of the protective paper that lined every exam table I'd ever been on. "I'm going to start with a couple of basic checks. Nothing too stressful."

Easy for him to say. You'd think after years of "basic tests" I'd be bored by them. Instead, as each year progressed and with every specialist the immunologist who coordinated my treatments consulted with, the same battery of tests were repeated to the point they'd become something stressful to be endured. I tried to keep my breathing smooth and even as he clipped a disposable top on the ear thermometer. There was no pain, of course, but the cold plastic being inserted into my ear canal was a violation that made my insides run cold.

A few seconds later, the device beeped and Dr. Weyer scanned the display. "Temp's 101. Excellent."

That got my attention. "Excellent? Why is a fever excellent?"

"Fever? Yusuf—"

"Call me Joey," I interrupted. For some reason I didn't mind when Owen called me by my real name, but it seemed weird, or wrong, whenever anyone else did.

He nodded. "Joey. Shifters in general, and big cats in particular, have a higher body heat than a human. A temperature of 101 is perfectly in range for you."

It took me longer than it should have for what he said to register completely. My parents, and every doctor I'd ever seen, had obsessed about my "feverish" temperature. For years. And he wanted me to believe it was, in his words, perfectly in range? How many tests had been run on me? How many treatments had been attempted to regulate my body temperature?

"But—" My voice cracked and I had to swallow past a fist-sized lump in my throat to breathe correctly.

The door crashed inward, and Owen burst in, an industrial-sized box of protein bars in one hand and a gallon milk jug in the other.

My mouth began to water. As soon as Owen was within reach, I grabbed the gallon of milk, twisted the top off, and started chugging. After I'd emptied half the jug and lack of breath had me dizzy, I pulled away, gasping. "Damn, why is that so good?"

Both Owen and Dr. Weyer gaped.

I wiped the back of my hand across my mouth. "Um, sorry about that. I've always had a thing for milk. There was about half a year when I was younger when my doctor assigned a no-dairy diet, thinking lactose intolerance might have been causing some of my problems."

"A dairy-free diet isn't practical for shifters."

I shrugged, glancing at Dr. Weyer. "Yeah, well, I don't think my doctor suspected I had an inner-lion thingy. He tried a lot of things. Once he prescribed a vegetarian, then a vegan, diet plan. That was after the dairy-free. Then there was a low-carb thing, then gluten-free. Last year he went with a paleo plan."

"Why?" Owen inspected my body in the baggy, yet too short for me, sweats. "You're too skinny as it is. Why would they have you on a diet?" As if to emphasize the statement, he passed me one of the protein bars.

"It wasn't a weight thing." I tore open the square packaging, revealing the dense brown bar inside. It didn't look very appetizing, even if the wrap claimed it had real apricot inside. "I've been sick most of my life. Symptoms always changed, but it's definitely been a chronic thing. When all the tests came back negative or inconclusive, he tried managing some of the symptoms through very specific diet plans. He ruled out Celiacs, for example, when the gluten-free diet had no impact on my symptoms." I crammed half the protein bar into my mouth. I really was hungry, and luckily my stomach hadn't rebelled yet. Especially with half a gallon of two percent in my belly.

"I think that's the most you've ever said at one time." Owen unwrapped another protein snack and handed it to me. He looked awed.

I paused my reach for the other bar. "Oh. Um… yeah. Maybe?"

Dr. Weyer didn't seem impressed by my unusual word-vomit. "Sick? What kind of sick? And what kinds of tests?"

I took another swig from the milk jug before shrugging like it was no big deal. "Pretty much you name it, they tried it. In the end, the closest anyone was able to come to a real diagnosis is some form of autoimmune disease."

"Autoimmune? Sounds pretty serious." Owen placed his hand on my knee. Even through the thick fabric of the sweatpants, I could feel his warmth, his energy, seeping into me. Added to it, my skin seemed to be extra sensitive, like whatever the whole shifter thing was had activated new nerves. Goose bumps spread over my body, and I shivered.

"And your parents let you leave for school, given what you were—are—going through?" Owen asked.

I snorted. "I didn't give them a choice."

"In what way?" Dr. Weyer asked.

"I didn't wait for their permission," I said simply. At his disapproving fatherlike look, I got a little defensive. "Look, I've been sick for years, undergone every test anyone has ever heard of. Nothing was helping. I decided I wasn't going to spend the rest of my life as a test subject. Since nothing was fixing it, I was just going to have to deal with it. Live with it. And since I'm of age and mentally competent, no one could force me to see another doctor. So sometimes I ache. Sometimes I have headaches. Sometimes it's worse. I'll deal with it, but I'm going to do it on my terms."

"Yusuf—sorry, Joey," Dr. Weyer corrected himself. "Will you give me access to your medical records? I'd like to take a look."

"I guess. But why? I mean, no offense, but I've been to nearly every specialist in the country already."

"Well, two reasons. First, it's important someone local is aware of your history in case an emergency comes up. And second, maybe more importantly, as a shifter and a doctor, I might have some insight the human doctors don't have."

My stomach lurched and the milk I'd slammed jostled sickeningly in my gut. Sharing a bit about my medical history had distracted me from the earlier insanity. But now it was time for some answers. "Yeah… there's that word again. Human. And shifter. And then there's the fact I turned into some kind of scrawny lion."

The two Weyer men looked to each other.

"Seriously," I said. "What's a shifter? And since when do men turn into bears and then back again?"

"So you've never heard of shifters before?" Doubt colored Dr. Weyer's tone.

"No. Why is that weird?"

"When your parents adopted you, didn't they—"

I jerked up my head, cutting him off. "Whoa. Adopted? I wasn't adopted. What the hell are you talking about?" My heart beat quickly, almost as quickly as when I'd morphed from paralyzed-on-the-ground human to terrified cat. My vision started to do that fade-to-green thing too.

Strong hands clamped down on both sides of my face. "Breathe, Yusuf. Deep breaths."

I closed my eyes and tried to focus on his campfire-at-midnight voice. After a long count to ten, I opened my eyes and met Owen's concerned gaze. He'd stepped close. So close, in fact, he took up the open space between my spread legs, our chests nearly touching. Dr. Weyer had a white-knuckled grip on Owen's shoulder and looked to be trying to pull him away. Owen didn't budge, though. He swiped his thumb along my cheekbone. "There you go. Relax."

I swallowed, nodded. After another moment, he stepped back.

"You take too many risks," Dr. Weyer snapped.

"He wouldn't hurt me," Owen said.

"You can't know that."

"I won't hurt him." My voice cracked a bit as I said the words, but I meant them. There was no way I'd hurt Owen, no matter what happened to me.

Neither Weyer said anything, but the elder released his hold on Owen's shoulder.

"If I promise to keep control, can you explain about the 'adopted' comment?"

Dr. Weyer tugged the hem of the simple white short-sleeved button-down he wore. "Simple genetics. Genetics and deduction. Being a shifter is inherited. You're a shifter, ergo your parents must be shifters. If they were shifters, they would never have subjected you to the tests they did." He paused, searching my expression for something. "I take it you didn't know you were adopted?"

"I'm not adopted. There's no way. I mean, my dad's Caucasian, my mom's Iranian. I'm clearly a mix between the two. There's got to be another explanation." I searched frantically for some other—any other—explanation. "Some of the tests were experimental. Maybe they, I don't know, triggered something."

Dr. Weyer shook his head. "I'm sorry. You are clearly a shifter, which means your parents—or at least one of your parents—are shifters. It's possible only one of your parents is a shifter. It might explain why you've gone so long before shifting."

"But wouldn't I know if one of my parents was a shifter? I don't think I'd have missed a three-hundred-pound feline roaming the house."

He just looked at me, sympathy shining in his amber eyes.

"You have to be wrong," I said. If they weren't wrong, it meant one or both of my parents had been lying to me my whole life. Or they weren't my parents after all. "You have to be wrong." I repeated the words, but they'd lost some of their conviction. "You're wrong."

AN hour later, Owen walked me back to Matthison Hall. We didn't speak. I was stuck in some kind of dazed out-of-body existence. The word *why* churned in my brain, stuck on repeat. Why me? Why now? Why was this happening? Why why why why.

I shivered. Admittedly it was a little chilly in the predawn air. Cody's high elevation meant that early mornings could often be jacket weather, even in July. But my shivers had less to do with temperature than shock. On the whole, I figured I'd handled everything okay. I mean, sure, I'd turned into some kind of lion and then commenced chuffing, hissing, and snarling at people when I was cornered. But who wouldn't? And, yeah, maybe it was easier to focus on me turning into a fucking cat than to wonder if my parents had lied to me my whole life. Because, of the two, betrayal by my parents was even more unthinkable than the existence of human-to-animal shape-shifters.

Another shiver racked my body, so I crossed my arms over my chest, gripping my opposite elbows tight.

Owen reached over and pried one of my hands free. He laced our fingers together, letting our linked hands dangle between us. A little of the tension crushing my heart eased. Not a lot. Not completely. But enough so I could breathe.

The sun peeked up from behind the Tetons to the east, a neon orange-and-pink halo brightening the sky. I sighed and let the peace of the moment—a breathtaking dawn and Owen's hand in mine—soak in.

Jesus, I was tired. I retreated deeper into my mind, trusting Owen to get me where I needed to be.

Chapter Six

THE *thud* of a fist pounding on my door dragged me out of my hundredth read-through of a beat-up paperback of *Watership Down*. Anthropomorphized rabbits had a whole new meaning now I knew human-animal shape-shifters existed. Now I knew I was one.

I squinted at the alarm clock on my bedside table. Three a.m.

"C'mon, Yusuf. I know you're awake. Open up." Owen's voice was quiet, but even through the sturdy door I could hear him clearly. In the two weeks since my foray into the wild side, improved hearing was only one of many changes I'd noticed. Hearing, sight, scent. Heck, things even tasted different. More acute, somehow.

I swung my legs over the side of my bed but hesitated before I could stand. I'd been avoiding Owen.

I wasn't altogether sure I was ready to face him. Not yet. Maybe not ever.

"Stop being an ostrich."

Despite myself, I grinned. "Ostrich?"

"Yeah. Burying your head in the sand. Avoidance isn't the answer. Besides," he added, "it's a waste of time. We're going to talk tonight, one way or the other. And I have the master key."

"That's a total misuse of your authority," I told him, even as I got to my feet and crossed my small dorm room to the door.

"I wouldn't have to use it if you weren't avoiding me."

I rested my hand on the knob, pausing. He didn't sound upset. In fact, patience more than irritation colored his voice. I had been avoiding him, yes. Though I supposed it was more accurate to say I'd been avoiding anything and everything having to do with my new reality. Including Owen. I needed time to wrap my head around everything that had happened and the consequences.

Maybe Owen was right. Avoidance was a waste of time. I swung the door open.

Compassion blazed in his golden amber gaze, and I crossed my arms over my chest, feeling more exposed than if I were naked. "Hey."

He placed his hand on my shoulder. Squeezed. "How're you doing?"

I nearly broke down. I'd been asked the same question a thousand times. Probably many thousands of times. Every day by my parents. By nurses. By doctors. By anyone and everyone I interacted with at any level. *How are you? How are you doing today?* Or, worse, *How are we doing today?* As if my illness was a communal experience. But tonight, with that one question and full of his damned compassion, I cracked. I didn't want to say "fine" or "okay" or whatever socially acceptable answer was expected. I wanted to be honest, to lay it all out for him, to dump every bit of panic and betrayal and doubt on him.

The most fucked-up part? I *was* fine. For the first time in my entire freaking life, I was physically fine. There were no aches, no pains. No blinding headaches or gut-twisting nausea. No mystery rashes, inflamed joints, or swollen lymph nodes. After nearly two decades of pain ranging from mild discomfort to excruciating, I was healthy as a horse.

But instead of dumping all that on Owen's doubtlessly capable shoulders, I shrugged. "I'm all right."

He shook his head. "No, you're not. It's okay to be freaked-out, you know."

"Thanks for the permission." I flopped back onto my bed. Then cringed. "Sorry. I shouldn't snap at you."

Owen waved it away. "No worries. Seriously, I get it. It's a lot to take in. But you're not going to do yourself any favors by dealing with it alone." He pulled the chair away from my desk and straddled it, his front against the back. "You should talk to someone, someone to help you figure everything out."

"And that someone is you?" I pulled one of the pillows away from the wall and clutched it to my chest. A fluffy barrier, but it was better than nothing. Not that I really thought I needed armor—not even emotional armor—between Owen and me. But the topic… it was a whole different kind of danger.

"If I gave you a name of someone else, would you talk to them? A professional? One who also is a shifter, because obviously talking to a human shrink might be problematic."

I just stared at him.

"I didn't think so. Which means you get me."

"Are you a shrink now?" I cringed again after I said it. Damn it, it wasn't like me to be mean. And I didn't lash out at people. "Sorry," I muttered, meaning it.

Again, Owen shrugged off my bad temper. "Almost. Or maybe it's more accurate to say someday."

I cocked my head.

"Psych major. Going for a PhD in clinical psychology. So, you know, someday."

I realized this was the first bit of personal information I really had about him. Sure, we'd hung out some for a while, but all I knew about him was his chess strategy and that his dad was a doctor. I hadn't asked, and he hadn't offered. On the other hand, he hadn't really asked me too many personal questions either. Had he read me so well he knew I wouldn't appreciate it? Or had I been so standoffish he hadn't felt comfortable?

"Oh." I clasped the pillow tighter to my chest.

His expression, not hard to begin with, softened further. "Seriously, relax. I don't plan on forcing you into some kind of therapy. But when you stopped coming down at night, I got worried. Also," he said with a spark of enthusiasm, "I found something." He leaned back in the chair to dig into the front pocket of his khaki shorts. The movement hiked up the hem of his blue-and-white-checked shirt, and through the slats of the chair back I caught sight of tight, tawny skin and a smattering of light brown hairs. I had a sudden urge to reach out and see what that skin-hair combo felt like under my fingers.

I tore my gaze away when he brandished his phone. "I figured out what your shift is."

I blinked, trying to rein in my wandering thoughts. "My shift?"

"Yeah. It's sort of a generic term for the animal we shift into."

"Okay. I take it you don't think I'm actually a lion?"

He grinned. "Close but no cigar."

"I have no idea what that means."

He rolled his eyes, his smile widening. "It might be a Wyoming saying. Who knows? But what I mean is you're a lion, but not an African lion. Not like the ones we see all the time."

I sorted through the random animal-related trivia I knew after two decades of Animal Planet and *National Geographic*. Something was there, on the outer edges of memory. I couldn't quite grasp it.

Owen shoved his phone at me. "An Asiatic lion."

I took the device automatically and focused on the picture there. It was definitely lionlike but different enough to seem like a distant cousin rather than a brother. Like the reflection in the windows of Matthison Hall that night, this lion—this Asiatic lion—had had a shorter mane, darker fur, with speckles. I think my reflection had been a bit scrawnier than the animal on the screen.

Without asking permission, I found a browser on Owen's phone and typed "Asiatic lion" into the search bar. Clicking open the first link to display, I skimmed the info it revealed.

Owen left the chair and slid next to me on the bed. He pointed at one of the paragraphs. "See, a lion, linked, but one that evolved differently."

"But they're from India. I'm Iranian."

"The natural lions live in India. Doesn't mean the shifter versions had to have come from India."

The reminder, not that I was apparently able to shift, but about where my family came from, was a punch to the gut. It made me think about my family and the fact that if Dr. Weyer was correct, I'd been lied to for years. It was that fact I'd been trying so hard to avoid. I didn't want to face it, to think about it. I passed the phone back to Owen and clutched the pillow even tighter.

Owen scooted back a bit to give me room, but he didn't leave my bed. He tucked his phone away and watched me for a moment before saying, "I take it you haven't asked your parents yet?"

I laughed, a mix of bitterness and weariness filling the sound. "How do I call the people who have loved me more than anyone or anything else in the world, who have sacrificed so much for me, even when I resented them for the coddling, to ask if they've been lying to me the whole time? If I was adopted, why wouldn't they have told me? If one of them is a shifter, why wouldn't they have said something?"

"I don't have a good answer for you. You'd know better than me what to expect from them. But I do know you won't get any answers if you don't ask the questions."

I slumped. "I don't want to hurt their feelings. I love my parents, I do. I know it might seem weird after I moved halfway across the country to get away from them, but it doesn't mean I don't care." I sounded a little desperate, like I was trying to convince myself.

"Of course not." We sat there in silence for a while.

"I've got an idea," he said, slapping the top of his thighs in a matter-of-fact way. "The way I see it, there are a few avenues for our search."

"*Our* search?"

Owen grinned. "Sure. You don't think I'm going to let you have all the fun?"

I wasn't sure I considered parental betrayal and a secret heritage fun, but since brooding in my room for the last two weeks hadn't gotten me any closer to answers or acceptance, working with someone couldn't hurt. Owen could provide a nice buffer between me and the reality I wasn't sure I was ready to face.

Part of me also recognized that the last couple of weeks not hanging out with Owen nearly every day made the loneliness harder to bear. I'd never been social, and with most interpersonal interactions restricted to my parents and medical staff nearly my entire life, I thought I'd long gotten used to my own company. But after having interacted with people my own age, solitude hung heavily across my shoulders and worse, in my head. I still went to classes, so technically I wasn't alone, but the emotional distance I'd built up the last several years—the shield that had started to thin after meeting Owen—had been strengthening, even harder and more impregnable than before.

"What did you have in mind?"

Owen angled his chin toward my desk, where my laptop sat next to an open textbook. "Can we use your computer?"

"Sure." I levered myself up to unplug the machine. The battery was fully charged, so we could stay lounging on the bed. When I situated myself back where I'd started, the mattress shifted under my weight, and I half fell into Owen. For a moment, just a tiny speck of a moment, I let myself lean against him. The solid presence of him next to me was both comforting and thrilling. I had no way to reconcile those contradictory sensations, so I passed the MacBook to Owen, then scooted back until a few inches separated us. I immediately missed his warmth.

After a quickly raised eyebrow, Owen located the web browser and started typing. "The way I see it, there are a few directions we can take. We can search online adoption records, see if anything pops."

I didn't like that option. Mostly because I didn't want to admit to the real possibility my parents weren't my biological parents, which would lead down a path of lies and distrust I didn't want to deal with.

"And since you're not comfortable going to your family…?" His voice trailed off even as the pitch in the last syllable hooked up, making it a question.

I shook my head. "I think, if I approach them… I think I need something more… some kind of evidence that doesn't involve me turning into an Asiatic lion."

"That's pretty irrefutable proof that they've kept something from you, one way or the other."

"I'm still not a hundred percent convinced it's not some kind of mutation or anomaly, maybe brought on by all the testing and drug therapies I was subject to growing up."

I could tell he wanted to say more, but instead Owen hit Enter on the keyboard with a flourish. "Which brings us to this option. We'll work our way back from the shifter part of you. Starting with the database."

"There's a shifter database? And it's online?" That didn't seem like a good way to keep under the radar.

"There is. And it is." Owen tilted the computer so I could see the screen. "And it's buried so deeply under layers of sites, and a sign-on and password is required to access it, that no one who isn't authorized gets far enough to even be curious."

The site he brought up wasn't fancy. In fact, it was basically a list of links and descriptions. As best as I could tell, it was sorted by country, by general type—canine, feline, bovine, avian—and then by individual species. "Is this like a directory?"

Owen nodded. "It's like a census and the Yellow Pages rolled into one. We've got demographic data, migration data, location data, and even contact information for some." He typed "lion" into the search bar, then scanned the results. The first page had a few dozen rows of *Panthera leo*.

"Are those individual shifters?" There weren't very many.

Owen scrolled through the lines. "Mostly family groupings. Prides, actually, since these are lions."

Families. There were at least a few dozen lion-shifter families. I peered closer at the screen, catching the snow-at-midnight and pinesap scents coming off Owen. I inhaled deeply, pressing closer before I remember what I was doing. Clearing my throat, I pointed at a middle column. Botswana. Cameroon. Kenya, Tanzania. The list was made up almost entirely of African countries, though I did see one listing in the United Kingdom and one in the US. "So this is where the shifter families live?"

"Yeah. I mean, shifter families move around and immigrate just like human groups. It's harder for some groups, though. A lion wandering through a nature preserve in Cameroon would draw a lot less attention than a lion wandering around the Tetons. So some groups tend to stay in the same general vicinity of their natural origins."

I didn't know what I was hoping to find. On the one hand, if we found there were lion-shifter families in or near Iran, it would be one step closer to indicating a parental betrayal rather than a medically induced mutation.

We scanned the second page of lion-shifter families. All were still located primarily in Africa, with only a couple of outliers. The tension pressing around my heart started to ease. None of the *Panthera leo* groups were settled anywhere near Iran. No lion shifters in Iran and only two families in the US.

Owen clicked to the next page. There, listed at the bottom, were three families of *Panthera leo persica*. Asiatic lions. Two families were located in India. One was located in Iran.

When Owen's hand hesitated, I reached over and clicked the link.

North Khorasan province.

An icy punch to the gut stole my breath and stopped my heart. Damn it.

Chapter Seven

I STARED dumbly at the damning words. Okay. It didn't have to mean anything. It was a coincidence. Nothing more. Except that particular coincidence struck a little too close to home. Or, more specifically, too close to my mother's home.

My hand shook as I reached over and slammed the lid of the laptop closed.

Owen covered my hand with his. "Yusuf?"

"It doesn't mean anything. It can't." My voice cracked. I jerked my hand free, grabbed the computer, and after jumping from the bed, I deposited the MacBook on the desk with less care than I probably should have. My eyes burned, pressure built in my chest, and I wanted to throw up. All physical reactions owing to the maelstrom of emotions building inside me. Betrayal and fear top among them. I clenched my fists, trying to rein in my emotions.

A subtle shift in the air behind me was the only sign Owen had followed me. Then his arms wrapped around me, strong and sure. At first I stood there, posture rigid. He didn't back off. If anything, he squeezed tighter, resting his forehead at the top of my spine. In this position the difference between our heights was more pronounced. That connection—that touch—destroyed the protective shields I was so desperately trying to shore up.

With a sob I spun around and buried my face in his hair. I clasped Owen to me, digging my hands into the cotton of his T-shirt.

He didn't say anything.

I didn't need him to.

I didn't say anything. I didn't have the words.

Instead, he held me while I let the tears flow, probably dampening his hair.

If I didn't know better, I'd have sworn he pulled the sharpest edges of my emotions away from me, siphoning them off. After a moment I finally found the words. "Why would they lie to me?"

He started rubbing my back, long strokes along my spine. "I can't say."

I pushed aside the thought that he was petting me and I was leaning into it like any Labrador would. Or a pet cat. I wanted it too much. Or maybe I needed it. Either way, I soaked up the contact. "I don't know what to do next."

"Are you sure you don't want to ask your parents? It's probably the simplest way."

I took half a step back. Enough to put a few inches of space between us, but not enough to break the connection of his hold. I wasn't ready for that yet. He didn't get it. I wasn't even sure I got it completely.

"I—I can't. I know it doesn't make sense, but I don't want to hurt them."

"And you think asking them will hurt them?"

"If I bring it up, it's like saying I don't trust them. And I do. But you've got to understand how the last few years have been."

"Tell me."

"I've been sick pretty much my whole life. The last few years, things got worse. Not the symptoms, though those were bad enough. But they tried so hard to figure it out. We had money. We weren't wealthy by any means, but my dad had an excellent salary and my mom had some kind of inheritance. It should have been enough to live more than comfortably, with plenty left over. With all my hospital time, Mom had to quit her job. Taking care of me was a 24-7 deal. Pretty soon, my dad's company started giving him a hard time over all the sick leave he was taking so he could shuttle me from one out-of-town doctor's appointment to the next. So Dad quit his job as a continuous improvement manager for an international manufacturing company to work from home as a consultant. It gave him more flexibility to be with Mom and me, but it also meant his income was cut almost in half."

Owen and I hadn't moved from our loose embrace in the middle of my dorm room. He hadn't released me, and I hadn't let go of him. If anyone walked in, we probably looked like we were frozen in the middle of a slow dance. He didn't seem anxious to move, and I knew I'd take advantage of every second. His eyes stayed open, which gave me the wherewithal to keep going. Maybe if I got the guilt off my chest, I'd be able to move forward.

"In over fifteen years, I don't think they took a single vacation. Their life revolved almost a hundred percent around me. After a while we'd gone through the battery of standard tests and therapies with no results, so they started looking into alternative treatments."

"Like acupuncture?"

I snorted. "I wouldn't knock acupuncture if I were you. We did that too, and it actually seemed to help with some of the aches and pains, at least for a short time. No, I mean like experimental."

He stiffened. "Experimental?"

"Yeah. They became experts at identifying any clinical trials and promising treatment plans abroad. The thing is, it was all really expensive. Between the travel and the experimental treatments not covered by insurance, they ran out of money."

"They love you. I'm sure it is worth it to them."

My heart twisted. "Yeah, so Dad said. Even as they sold the house and downsized into a condo. It didn't matter to them. I was what mattered."

He trailed his hand down my spine again. "They're your parents. Of course that's what they think. Wouldn't you do the same for them?"

I nodded. "Yeah. But how can I, after all their sacrifices, accuse them of keeping something so major away from me? I mean, I'm either adopted, or one or both of my parents are Asiatic lion shifters. I don't want to sound ungrateful." I was getting dangerously close to repeatedly circling the same point.

"I don't know what to tell you. My relationship with my own parents isn't the same."

Something in his voice pulled me out of my immobilizing pity party. It wasn't resentment or anger. Maybe resignation? The words themselves could have meant anything. But the tone. "Everything seemed cool between you and your dad the other night."

"Oh, things are fine." He rocked his head from side to side as though loosening the joints. "We get along fine. We're just not as closely connected as it sounds like your family is."

He stepped away from me, dropping his arms to his sides. I tried not to mourn the missing warmth.

"Anyway," he said, jamming his hands into his pockets, "you should try to get some sleep. It'll be easier to concoct a plan after a few z's."

My lips twisted in an involuntary, if bitter, smile. "You're kidding, right? Hadn't you noticed I don't sleep much?"

The emotional shield he'd put between us cracked a little, and his gaze softened. "Yeah. Even if you hadn't visited me in the overnight shifts, those dark circles under your eyes would tell me. But still, you need sleep. So try. Tomorrow will be soon enough to plan our next step."

He turned to step toward the door, but I stopped him with a hand on his arm. "Thanks, Owen." When he looked at me curiously, I added, "For not letting me play the ostrich."

"You're welcome." He leaned in and brushed his lips over mine. It lasted barely a second, was butterfly soft, and ended much too quickly. Before the action had time to register, it was done, and Owen was gone.

I pressed my fingertips to my still-tingling lips. And he expected me to go to sleep?

I RESTED my head on my palm and tried to keep my gritty eyes focused on Dr. Coleman. We'd started a new chapter on the politics of wildlife management. Any other time I'd have been completely absorbed in the materials and his lecture. Maybe it was because of how young he was, but he was completely engaging, even when talking politics. It may not have been ornithology, which was his main passion, but he managed to make even legislative finagling interesting.

Most of the time.

Today I was too tired and way too distracted to keep up with the partisan views on property rights and preservation. And for the first time since the full moon, it had nothing to do with my inner lion. No, it had everything to do with Owen's kiss.

Which was ridiculous. It was barely a brush. No more intimate than kissing a cousin. Or a maiden aunt.

But it was my first kiss. And it was Owen.

I'd already figured out guys kind of did it for me. Mostly thanks to Owen. But discovering a homosexual— or maybe bisexual, I hadn't dug too deep into that well of self-discovery yet—component to myself was secondary to discovering I had a lion inside me. A fucking lion!

But that kiss.

Honestly, it could barely be called a kiss. It was a peck. A buss. A smooch. No, not a smooch. I wasn't five. But still.

For more than an hour after he'd left, my mind repeated this stupid cycle. And when it wasn't busying coming up with every synonym I could find for *kiss*, my mind provided a lovely image of Owen performing different variations of the kiss—a hand kiss, a forehead kiss, a french kiss. Which had me imagining Owen's mouth on me in all sorts of other tantalizing places. Which had me twitchy and sweaty and hard. It wasn't that I'd never had an erection before, but with everything else going on with my body, it hadn't happened often.

Suddenly, with one brief touch and several years' worth of catching up to do, I had a lion-sized libido and no idea what to do with it.

All because of a stupid, platonic brush of his lips that probably didn't mean anything more to him than a handshake would have. Or a hug. Or a slap on the back.

And, damn it, I needed to let it go and deal with the rest of the crap in my life.

"Joey?" Someone touched my shoulder, and I jerked, sending my laptop skittering to the edge of my desk. I barely managed to slam my hand down—probably cracking a couple of keys—in time to keep the computer from crashing to the floor.

I looked up to see the empty classroom and Dr. Coleman standing next to me. I squeezed my eyes shut. Class was over, and I'd missed the exodus of students. "Sorry," I muttered, pulling my shoulder bag to my lap. I dumped everything into it, not even bothering to save my notes or power down my laptop.

"You okay?" Dr. Coleman asked.

"Yeah, I'm fine. Sorry I zoned out there for a bit."

Instead of looking pissed that I'd basically ignored the last twenty minutes of his lecture, he looked concerned. He tucked his thumbs into the pockets of his khaki pants. His red polo shirt matched his Converse high-tops, something I only noticed because I was avoiding meeting his eyes. "You sure you're okay? You look a little rough around the edges."

It was a generous way to put it. I looked like I hadn't slept in two weeks, which I guess I hadn't. "I'm fine. Long night." After my first—and hopefully only—shift, I'd started feeling and looking healthier. But restless sleep and tossing and turning would leave anyone a little rough around the edges.

Dr. Coleman nodded. "Well, try to get some sleep. And reread chapter six to catch back up. There's going to be a quiz on what we covered today."

I sighed, humiliated and grateful at the same time. It was not a comfortable feeling. "Thanks. And I promise to pay attention tomorrow."

"It's no big deal. It happens to the best of us." He moved back to the front of the room and started packing up his stuff.

I shot a quick glance over my shoulder as I exited the room. Dr. Coleman really was a pretty cool guy. I thought about what the girl had said that day at lunch. He didn't seem like the kind of guy to hook up with his TA. He came across as the kind of guy who'd be more likely to tutor the jock and fantasize about him from a distance.

A tall guy with more than a little Native American in his features strode past me, his elbow-length black hair swinging behind him. There was nothing visible, but I swore energy crackled around him, and I smelled ozone and coffee in his wake. More, I sensed power unlike anything I'd ever felt before. I stopped in my tracks, heart beating in an irregular rhythm as my fight-or-flight instincts battled it out again. The man was a predator, no doubt about it. And I would bet any amount of money he was a shifter too. The guy must have seen or felt my stare, because he shot a look my way before entering the classroom I'd just left.

Distantly, I heard Dr. Coleman say, "Hey, babe."

He was Dr. Coleman's ex-TA? The geeky bird-nerd professor hooked up with... words failed me. Clearly, the ornithology professor was more badass than I'd have guessed.

I left the Reynolds Sciences building, brain fuzzy from lack of sleep and awe at Dr. Coleman's balls, which is why it took me so long to register my name after I'd gone half a block in the direction of the dorms.

"Yusuf!"

Blinking, I turned to Owen, who was jogging up behind me. Just like that day I had lunch with "the guys."

"Déjà vu," I murmured, my stomach twisting greasily. Then I recalled a moment in my dreams where Owen had used his hands to…. My stomach dropped to my knees. My face burned, and my mouth dried. I couldn't face him. Not now. Not after picturing him like that.

Oblivious to my discomfort, Owen stepped close and smiled. "You're done with class for the day, right?"

I licked my lips. I could do this. I could be normal. Or at least not act like a complete moron. "Ah, yeah. I'm heading to my room." I pointed lamely to Matthison Hall, as if Owen didn't know exactly where it and my room were located.

"You have plans for lunch?"

"Lunch?" I said the word like I'd never heard it before. I was making this whole thing more awkward than it had to be, and if I didn't relax, Owen was going to notice. And if he asked, what would I say? *Ever since you kissed me, I've developed an oral fixation. I want you to kiss and lick and suck me all over. I know you didn't mean it like that, but there you have it.* Yeah, so there was no way I could tell him the truth. Better if he didn't ask. "Lunch," I repeated more decisively. "No. No plans for lunch." See, I could play it cool.

"Good. There's someone I want you to meet." Owen rested his hand on my back, nudging me the opposite direction from where I'd been heading, which would have been fine, but he didn't move his hand when we were clearly going the way he wanted us to go.

I concentrated on watching for cracks in the sidewalk instead of the heat from his palm on my spine. "Where are we going and who are we meeting?"

"There's a café on the next block, Buddy's. We're meeting a friend of mine. Okay, he's not really a friend, more of an ex, but I think he'll be able to help with your situation."

His ex? I couldn't possibly meet one of his exes. Not while fantasies of Owen still lingered in my brain.

Then the more pertinent part of his statement sank in. Help. He thought his ex could help with my situation.

"Help? In what way?"

Owen bit his lip. Like I needed any more reason to obsess about his mouth. "He's sort of a, you know, a hacker."

"A hacker?"

"Well, actually, he's a journalism major, a senior, who does a little hacking on the side."

"A little hacking." My voice came out breathy, and I sounded more than a little incredulous.

"He's not a criminal or anything," he rushed to reassure me. "At least, he didn't used to be. Mostly he just does research. Sometimes he digs a little deeper than maybe he should. He wants to be one of those investigative journalists, the ones who uncover major stories."

I cleared my throat. "Um, like those Watergate reporters?" I didn't think my parental betrayal, or whatever it was, would require Woodward and Bernstein.

"Kind of. Someday, at any rate, though I think he's shooting to be the next Anderson Cooper. He's really good at digging up stuff people would rather stay buried."

"And he's your ex?" I cringed. I hadn't meant to say that. It was none of my business. It had no bearing on me or my situation.

Owen rubbed his palms along the thighs of his jeans. "Yeah. We went out for a while. Just didn't mesh. Nothing in common outside of sex. There wasn't any drama or anything. You don't have to worry about that. We're still, well, not friends, but friendly."

I forced myself to say, "Good. That's… that's good." Because it was good. Friendly was good. No drama was good. But really, the only thing I could focus on was the *nothing in common outside of sex* comment. I didn't want—or need—to know about Owen having sex with anyone else. In fact, it was all I could do to keep the feral growl building in my chest subdued.

My hands clenched and my fingertips tingled. A reminder, since I clearly needed it, that I had something much more pressing to worry about than what Owen did with some other guy way back when.

How do you know it was way back when? It might have been weeks, or even days, ago. I mentally squashed the little voice in my head. I didn't need that kind of thinking. I had more important details to deal with.

Chapter Eight

WHEN we walked into Buddy's and I saw the guy who stood up and waved, all my good intentions vanished. The guy was gorgeous. Tall, slim, nearly delicate in build, this guy—who Owen called David, though the actual introduction was lost in the static of rage and awe in my brain—had the kind of androgynous beauty that would make millions on runways. Smooth, milky skin stretched over sharp-edged cheekbones and a perfectly straight nose. His mouth was wide and perfectly bowed. Even his damn eyebrows were perfectly arched. He was, in a word, perfect. If I had to find a fault—and believe me, I *had to* find a fault—it would be that his rich auburn hair was a little too long, like he was maybe a few weeks past due for a trim. Physically, it was his only fault. If the dude got a haircut, he'd be, in a word, perfect.

Maybe I'd luck out and his voice would be squeaky or he'd be dumb as a post. Because, yeah, computer hackers and investigative journalists were always known for their dim wits. And then he opened his mouth. "Owen, it's great to see you." His voice was rich, smooth as his skin, and held a warm familiarity that had my inner lion pacing restlessly. I wanted to slash at David with my claws, tear into him with my teeth. The violence of my reaction scared me enough to mute the lion's aggression. At least a little bit.

Then David wrapped his arms around Owen.

I snarled. Audibly. In a public place.

David's lake-blue eyes—of course they were a glinting, sparkling blue; what other color could they possibly have been—widened.

Owen gaped.

I slapped a hand over my mouth, horrified. "Sorry," I said from behind my palm. "Don't know what happened." I took a step back. I needed a minute to gain some control over myself. "I'm going to get a latte. Can I get you something?"

Owen shook his head. "You should avoid the caffeine. Get water or juice or something."

It was my turn to gape. Was he seriously telling me what I should drink? "Excuse me?"

Searching my face as though he couldn't figure out why I was upset, Owen cocked his head. "You already have trouble with insomnia. Espresso will only make it worse."

It was a stupid thing to put my back up, but I'd worked too hard, risked too much, to be my own person and make my own decisions for me to easily give up even the smallest sliver of independence. "A latte ten hours before bedtime isn't likely to hurt me."

David watched us, undoubtedly filing away details for some kind of mental exposé. I could see it now: To Caffeinate or Not to Caffeinate—The Insomniac's Beverage Battle.

Owen reached out, hand gliding down my arm. I stepped away before his touch could weaken my resolve. "Also," he said quietly enough no one else should be able to hear him, "caffeine can have some weird effects on certain shifters. You should play it safe until you've had time to work with my dad."

"When am I working with your dad?"

"You'll have to work with someone to practice control. He'll be able to find a mentor, someone discreet."

"Why—"

"You snarled a minute ago, remember? And your eyes glowed for a second too. If you're going to be around nonshifters, you're going to have to learn control." He looked around carefully. "Also, my dad is researching your condition. He should be able to figure out how you managed to go over twenty years before shifting."

I pursed my lips. I hated that his arguments were sound. I especially hated that once again someone was trying to dictate my life. I'd already escaped from my overprotective family. Well-intentioned or not, I was tired of people arranging my life without my input.

"We'll talk about this later." I rolled my eyes toward David, who was still watching us like this was some kind of reality TV show.

I stalked to the front counter, where a girl with short dark hair and thick-framed glasses asked for my order. I read the menu board and its dozens of coffee drinks. Cursing silently, I ordered a mango-pineapple smoothie. My stomach seemed to be gnawing at my backbone, so the extra calories and protein from the smoothie would do me good. I grabbed a bottle of water for Owen. If I didn't get caffeine, neither did he.

I took advantage of the wait for my drink to rein in some of those primal reactions causing so much trouble. I had enough difficulties with other people trying to control my life; I didn't need these unfamiliar emotions and instincts driving me too.

By the time I walked back across the café, smoothie in hand, I'd managed to stuff the internal crap back down.

They'd found a table near the back, partly obscured by a floating bookshelf. Buddy's business was brisk, especially for midday, but even a nonshifter nose could have picked up the aroma of baked bread and simmering soup weaving through the coffee and chocolate smells I would normally associate with a café. The place had a rustic-cabin-meets-garage-sale chic look that was both homey and hip, and I could see myself bunkering down here when I needed to escape the dorms. Doing homework over there by the big stone fireplace appealed to me more than my room or the library. It would be especially nice, I decided, come winter.

I slid into one of the mismatched chairs next to Owen. I passed him the bottle of water. He eyed my smoothie but was perceptive enough not to indicate with even the flicker of an eyelash that it wasn't the latte I'd intended.

Needing to prove I wasn't an asshole driven entirely by animal instincts, I offered David my hand. "Sorry about earlier. Things have been... odd... for me lately. I'm Joey Franke."

David shook my hand and smiled. I had to make a conscious effort to not be dazzled by the perfection of it.

He was just so shiny. "Owen's told me a little about your situation. I can see how you might be a bit on edge."

I glanced at Owen, but my question was directed at David. "What exactly did he tell you?"

Owen answered. "I only told him what he needed to know to find the information we need."

"Can we trust him?" It was totally rude to talk about David as though he weren't watching us from the other side of the table, but it probably wouldn't hurt for him to know I wasn't going to accept him at face value.

"Yeah. As long as we're clear that he's got his hacker hat on and not his reporter one. He's good at not blurring those lines."

David snorted, apparently tired of passively observing. "Believe me, blurring those lines could get me into big trouble. Not like I'm going to advertise my less-than-legal skill set."

"It may not come to that," Owen rushed to assure him—or maybe me. "There are layers, and a lot of adoption information—if it applies," he added quickly when I hissed in objection, "is public record. David can do those kinds of searches faster and more comprehensively than either of us could."

I acknowledged his point even as my shoulders tightened. The idea of finding proof my parents were not biologically mine, that they'd been lying to me this whole time, had tension rising in me. "Only open adoptions are available publicly, right?"

Owen's lips twisted. "That's where the hacker part comes in."

My stomach dropped. I shot a look at David. "How illegal is it?"

"Very. There are lesser consequences if you were to break in and steal paper copies of the records than the internet-based data," he said wryly. "Especially since most states have legal channels for adopted children to request and receive their biological parents' information, even in closed adoptions. Since we're looking for verification rather than actual parent information, I wouldn't need to go that deep, so the risk of getting caught is less."

I pushed back from the table, the chair legs scraping roughly on the floor. "No. No, I don't want putting yourself at risk. Not about this. Not for me. Especially since I don't think there's any way I'm adopted. I mean, what are the chances a Caucasian and an Iranian would adopt a baby who is clearly a biracial mix of Caucasian and Persian ethnicity?"

Owen put his hand on my knee, and the panic receded. "Relax. I didn't—don't—expect things to go that far. I think we should do this in a few stages."

"Stages?" I asked.

"Figures," David said.

When I looked at him, he clarified. "Owen always has ideas and plans. He seems so laid-back and chill, but underneath he's plotting and planning. Do yourself a favor. Don't play chess with him."

I don't know which part of David's statement I disliked the most. There was definitely some bitterness in how obvious it was that David knew Owen better than I did. I'd never seen signs of him plotting or planning. But knowing David and Owen had played chess really rankled. A dark, selfish part of me treasured all those nights of chatting and chess. I wanted our time to have been special. Finding out it wasn't hurt nearly as much as coming face-to-face with Owen's picture-perfect ex-lover.

And I had no right to the jealousy in either situation.

Owen smirked. "Yusuf holds his own. Wins as often as he loses."

He sounded proud of me. I swore my inner feline purred in satisfaction.

This whole thing was ludicrous, so I pretended to ignore it. "So, stages?"

"Right. The way I see it, we have two angles we need to follow. The possible adoption and the shifter side. I think the first thing we should do is have David scan the public adoption records."

David dipped his chin. "Yeah, I can do that. I'll set up a search algorithm using your name, your birthday, your parents' names, see what pops. All perfectly aboveboard and legal."

"Theoretically, we could do a similar search too," Owen told me. "But we'd have to resort to random Google searches, so David's way will be faster. Then, or maybe while his search is going, we'll need to follow the shifter trail. That one will require hacking."

David leaned back in his seat. "You want me to hack the shifter database?" I caught a whiff of something mildly sour coming off him, a scent that wasn't there before. Nerves, the primal part of me suggested. I wasn't used to identifying emotions through my olfactory senses, but something, probably my inner lion, seemed capable of making the distinction.

David hadn't batted an eye at illegally digging through sealed adoption records, which potentially came with severe legal consequences. But breaking into the shifter database, which wasn't tied into any government agency, made him sweat? "Is that bad?"

"Yes."

"No. David's just being a wimp."

I looked at David, who glowered at Owen. His lips pursed, and his eyes narrowed. Definitely one of those "if looks could kill" scenarios. Owen acted oblivious to the deadly glare, raising his eyebrows expectantly.

David deflated. "Damn it, my mother will murder me."

"Only if you get caught."

It felt like they were speaking a foreign language or in code or something. "Your mother?"

He slumped in his seat. "She's the director of the Western division of the US Shifter Council."

"Which means you have easy access through the database's firewalls. Your job will be made much easier."

"Not from here, I don't. Maybe from my mother's system." Some of the dread left him, and he straightened his spine. Clearly he'd found an argument to counter Owen's request.

"You're going home for Fourth of July this weekend, right?"

David narrowed his eyes. "Bastard."

"Look, you can't tell me part of you isn't thrilled at the idea of seeing if you can get past your brother's programing."

"Evil, manipulative bastard."

Owen smiled, looking sweet and innocent, and very unbastardlike.

I probably looked confused. Owen took pity on me. "David's brother is a successful program developer. He specializes in security systems that are used by all sorts of important people."

"He's not that good." David rolled his eyes and crossed his arms over his chest.

"Here's your chance to prove it," Owen said.

Exhaling with loud *whoosh*, David sat up. "Fine. What information will I be risking my mother's wrath, possible incarceration, or even exile to collect?"

"Don't forget the bragging rights you'll be earning."

"There's that. Anyway, what are you looking for in the databases?" David reached behind him and pulled out a smartphone and a stylus, ready to take notes.

"There are three known prides of Asiatic lions. One in North Khorasan, Iran, one in Gujarat, India, and one in Madhya Pradesh, India. We need information about the prides. Kind of a who's who or a where-are-they-now search."

"If you know where the prides are, you've already accessed the database." David lifted his stylus.

"Yeah, we saw what was in the public view. Problem is, there's nothing there. Just the list of the locations, and it's completely generic. A basic list of the provinces or states where the prides are located, nothing more specific."

"Wait a minute." I jabbed a finger at Owen. "Is that weird? You didn't say anything about it last night."

"I needed to verify a few things. I didn't want to make more of it than it was, if they changed the system views or something. You had enough to deal with without adding to it unnecessarily."

"That wasn't your call—" I stopped myself. Now wasn't the time to object to his making decisions to "protect" me. I took a breath and started over. "I take it you verified there should be more data?"

"I looked up some other groups in other parts the country, and in other countries. Family and pride or pack listings typically include basic census data. Names, birthdates, addresses, the whole deal. The missing information is a little suspicious."

"Given the locations of Asiatic lions, though, it's possible—even probable—the prides are solitary. They may not interact with others or accept regular check-ins." David moved his stylus over the screen too fast for me to track.

"Which is what I want you to find out."

David nodded, tap-tap-tapping away. "Got it. I'm going to need info from you, Joey, before I can start the adoption records searches."

"Of course."

"While you two start, I'm going to hit the men's room." Owen pushed back his chair, then stood. "You should finish your smoothie. Maybe grab a sandwich."

I gave him my best deadpan look. "I don't need a babysitter."

He held up his hands. "Sorry."

He headed to the back of the café, where a wooden sign with the word Gents burned into it hung above a swinging door. I admired the way his khaki shorts showcased his ass and muscular thighs.

David cleared his throat. I whipped my head back to him, heat burning my cheeks.

"I don't blame you for looking, and Buddy's about as close to a safe space as you're going to find around here, but this is Wyoming."

The blood suffusing my face changed course and dropped to my knees. I hadn't thought about that. Not at all. I rubbed the back of my hand across my chin and mouth. "I guess I'm not in Chicago anymore," I said. Not like it had anything to do with being caught ogling some dude's ass. I wouldn't have done it in Chicago either. It was like my hormones had been on hiatus while my body struggled to figure itself out. And now…. But, yeah, I needed to watch myself.

Time to deflect. The condensation on my smoothie cup had made a little pool on the table. I mopped it up with a napkin, noticing I'd only finished about a third of it. "Why are you doing this, David?"

"This?"

"Yeah. Why would you spend your time, and take the risk, to help me figure this shit out? I'll be honest. I can't afford to pay you anything, and you don't know me from anybody."

"I know Owen. And he's really good at convincing people to help. Pretty sure he single-handedly recruited every volunteer for the Cody College Charitable 5K last spring. Even people who'd never volunteered for anything in their life found themselves donating their time."

"He told me you guys dated for a while." I mentally cringed. Shit. Why had I said that? "Sorry! I didn't mean to say anything. It's none of my business."

"Oh, I know why you mentioned it." His tone and his smile were sly. "But you don't need to worry about me. We gave things a go last year, but we were never a good match."

"But you were together?"

David shrugged. "Yeah, but I think it was one of those things that sounded like a better idea than it was. Our families are close, and it seemed like a natural pairing. He's nice and he's hot, but he's not for me. And I'm the wrong guy for him. So, yeah, the way is clear for you."

"I didn't... I'm not...." I sputtered. "Just, let's just move one."

His perfect smile flashed again. "Moving on. I'm going to need your full name, your parents' names, your birthday, birthplace—city and state, and if you know which hospital that would be, even better—your birthday."

"I was born in Tehran."

"Tehran? Iran?" David dropped his stylus. "That complicates things."

"How so?"

"I'm not even sure where to start looking. Maybe if I had the actual birth certificate. Is it an American certificate, at least? Or are you an Iranian citizen? Or dual citizenship? Can you have dual citizenship between the US and Iran?"

"Iran doesn't recognize dual citizenships. It wouldn't matter for me, though. My father is American, and he'd worked in Tehran for a while. My mother had a green card through her marriage to Dad. So I was born in Iran, but I'm an American citizen."

"That helps. There's bound to be records, then, from when they got your American birth certificate issued. Do you have the birth certificate with you?"

I shook my head. "My parents have it stored in their files."

He bit the side of his lip, focusing internally, like he had some kind of inner list he was reviewing. "Any chance you can get your hands on it? Or even a copy of it?"

"Maybe. If I told them I needed it for some financial aid forms or something." When I made my escape, I probably should have brought some of my files—or at least my birth certificate—along with me. I'd been afraid of losing something important. Of course, at the time I'd had no idea I'd be suspicious of my origins.

"Well, we'll get the rest of the info you know, and I'll start looking. But as soon as you can get me your birth certificate, or the exact time, date, and location of your birth, let me know, and I'll update the search parameters."

By the time Owen returned, David had taken down some of my information, then left, muttering something about algorithms and bots and other things I didn't understand.

Chapter Nine

I WAS as ready as I was going to be. I had a bulleted list of talking points. I'd rehearsed my request a dozen times. All I had to do was dial my phone. Easy, right? I mean, I didn't even have to dial any numbers. I only had to click an icon, or tell Siri to call my parents. No dialing required. But I'd been staring at my phone for the last twenty minutes.

I'd already put it off longer than I should have. First, I decided I couldn't do it without getting something for lunch first. A fruit smoothie wasn't a meal, after all. And, given I'd been eating twice as much as usual and I was still hungry, a little predeception meal was in order. Then I had to wait until after five. It wouldn't be fair to interrupt my dad at work, right? And I needed to charge my phone. Couldn't have the battery die at the wrong moment. Then I had to eat again, followed closely by the realization that my parents were likely doing their own thing for dinner, and I couldn't possibly interfere with their plans. Which was how I ended up staring at my fully charged phone, with its mocking green Call icon glowing at me. If I didn't make the call now, my parents would be in bed, and I'd have to deal with the stress and angst again all day tomorrow.

My thumb hovered over the icon. I took a deep breath—

Knock knock.

Son of a bitch. "Who is it?" I barked, slamming the phone onto my bed. My neatly made bed, because goodness knew I couldn't possibly call my parents from a rumpled, slept-in bed.

I didn't need his answer to tell me who was there. Even through the door, I could catch the edge of his midnight-in-flight, snow-and-fir scent. But normal people didn't generally identify their friends by scent, and I desperately needed to feel normal right now. *Normal* meant I wouldn't break down and confess all to my parents the minute they picked up the phone.

"It's me, Owen."

I sighed, then grabbed my phone as I stood to open the door. Maybe a little distraction would give me the guts to do what I needed to do.

The tinny ringing noise coming from my hand stopped me in my tracks.

Somehow, when I grabbed up my phone, I'd accidentally hit the stupid green Call button. The one so helpfully displayed below my parents' contact information.

"Oh shit." I stared at the phone like it was a bomb about to explode. Every nanosecond that passed was one nanosecond closer to the point of no return. I wasn't ready. This was enough to knock me off my game. Like, big-time.

"Yusuf?" Owen knocked at the door again. "Is everything okay in there?"

The call rang again.

Any second now my mom was going to answer.

I grappled at the door handle, remembered to unlock it, tried again.

Owen stood there, arm poised to knock once more.

The call rang again.

Maybe Mom wasn't there? I could hang up, but she'd see I called. If I didn't leave a message, or if I hung up without talking to her, she'd assume the worst. She'd probably have the Navy SEALs or the National Guard on campus in a matter of seconds. All while booking a flight and packing a bag. She was scarily efficient. And dramatic. And protective.

"Joey? Baby, is that you?"

And she'd answered the call.

Owen cocked his head, eyes wide with concern. "You okay?" he mouthed, stepping close and resting his hand on my shoulder.

And just like that, the nerves were siphoned off. I nodded to tell him I was okay, then lifted the phone to my ear. "Hey, Mom."

Owen moved as though to leave me to my call, but I grabbed his wrist to stop him. His presence, maybe the support in it, grounded me. I didn't know the why or how of it, but at this moment it didn't matter. I needed every bit of support I could get.

I dragged Owen to my bed, nudged him down, then sat next to him. I grabbed the notebook in which I'd jotted my talking points. Owen's eyebrow quirked at my notes, but he didn't say anything.

"It's been almost a month since we've talked! Your father was about to call the Marines."

I couldn't help but smile. My mother always used "your father" when she really meant "I." To hear her tell it, you'd think my father was a nervous wreck. Guilt quickly replaced the momentary flash of nostalgia. The month she claimed was a slight exaggeration, but I hadn't called since the week before my inner lion decided to introduce himself to campus. Since that night, I didn't have any idea what to say to my parents. Even if I avoided the elephant in the room—or would that be a lion in the room?—I was afraid she'd pick up on the doubt and fear. And if she thought something was wrong, there would be no stopping her. She'd be on the next flight west.

I'd paused too long, lost in my thoughts, because she started flinging questions at me in her lightly accented voice. "What's wrong? You've been sick, haven't you? I knew we shouldn't have let you leave. What are your symptoms? Should we call Dr. Mirza?"

"Sorry," I managed to say before she could spiral any further. "I'm fine, I promise. No need to call Dr. Mirza." I covered the speaker on my phone to clarify for Owen. "My immunologist."

"Who is with you?" Mom demanded. "Who are you talking to?"

Whoops. "My… friend is here." Damn it. My voice wasn't supposed to stumble on the word.

"Friend?" Mom asked. She made the word sound like a foreign concept. Which maybe it was. I'd never really called anyone "friend" before. And even my parents didn't have anyone they called friend. They'd been too caught up in me and my health crises to have much time for friendships away from the doctors. Just one more thing to add to the pile of stuff I felt guilty about.

I cleared my throat. "Yeah. His name is Owen."

"Well, that's good, isn't it? You have a friend."

She sounded a little odd. Was that hesitancy? Or pleasure? Damn the long-distance connection. It was so hard to read her emotions without seeing her face.

"So, um… sorry it's been so long since I've checked in. I've, um, been pretty busy lately. Classes, you know."

"But you're feeling well? Your father says Dr. Mirza received a request for your medical records."

Damn it, I'd forgotten I'd given Dr. Weyer permission to request my records. It hadn't occurred to me Dr. Mirza would have told anyone. I was pretty sure HIPAA laws should have prevented that. Of course, Dr. Mirza had been my specialist since I was five years old. He probably hadn't even considered the fact that I was no longer a minor before discussing things with my father.

That would explain the number of their calls I'd let go to voicemail over the last few days. Now I felt even worse for the radio silence. The records request probably sent up all sorts of red flags. "No, seriously, Mom, I'm fine. Really." I was teetering on a very thin line. I had to convince my parents I was well enough they didn't worry themselves into ulcers, but I couldn't let on how much better I truly was. That kind of swing on the health scale, even one for the better, would be cause for alarm. Especially since I couldn't explain the cure. Not yet, at any rate. Maybe not ever.

Owen tapped a finger on the notebook held forgotten in my hand.

Right. My talking points. I sucked in a steadying breath. I could do this. "Anyway, I need a favor."

"A favor?"

"Yeah. Can you send me my birth certificate?"

There was a pause, then, "Your birth certificate?"

"Yeah, I probably should have brought it with me, but I didn't realize I'd need it and I thought it would be safer in the files at the house. But now I need it, and I don't have it, so—"

Owen patted my thigh, causing the avalanche of words to tumble to a halt. I never babbled. It, as much as anything else, told me I was more keyed up than I'd ever been before. Owen's touch did more than stop the words, though. It also stopped my brain. Only momentarily, thankfully.

"Why do you need your birth certificate, Joey?"

My mind screeched to a halt.

"Joey?"

Owen nudged me. Crap. "Oh, uh, financial aid forms," I finally said after sputtering for a few seconds while my brain struggled to come back online.

"Financial aid forms?" Mom's voice sharpened. "Joey, what is the matter? I thought you had already taken care of your tuition payments."

I cringed. Just one more log to throw on the guilt fire. My parents had spent every penny they'd earned on my health care, tapping into their retirement funds and everything. But they hadn't stopped making regular deposits into my college fund. One I should have been too proud to touch. I wanted my independence; I should have done my damnedest to do it on my own. But I didn't have any obvious skills, and college was expensive, so I'd used part of the college fund to finance my education.

"I'm considering not using the fund you set up. You guys have done so much already, that, um, I was going to look into financial aid options so you guys could, I don't know, take a vacation."

Owen rolled his eyes.

My mother let out a horrified gasp. "Yusuf Robert Franke!" Then she started muttering something in Persian. The words were muffled, so I didn't quite catch what she was saying. It was probably better that way.

Ten minutes and a promise to contact my father later, I managed to calm my mom. She hadn't promised to send me my birth certificate. I tried not to let the omission mean anything more than it did. After I disconnected the call, I tossed my phone on my desk and returned to my bed. Owen had scooted himself against the wall on the bed, tucking his legs under him tailor-fashion.

"Dude, you are the worst liar. Like, ever."

I groaned and plopped down next to him. The mattress bounced, causing me to rock into Owen. Instead of his typical polo shirts, tonight he wore a tank top that showed off the breadth of his shoulders and the taut hills of his biceps. My arm pressed briefly against his, sending little zings of warmth skittering along my nerves. I'd ended up closer to him than I'd expected, and Owen probably wasn't looking for a snuggle buddy. I inched away so our bodies didn't touch.

"You're right. I'm a terrible liar. It's just that I've never really lied to them before. I mean, the occasional fib about whether I drank enough water, sure, but never an outright lie. I hate it." I pressed my fist to my queasy stomach. Yeah. The whole thing didn't sit well with me.

He reached over and rubbed along my back. I wanted to melt into the touch. It was comforting and disconcerting. "Figured. The bullet points gave it away. Most practiced liars don't need a script."

I slouched against the wall, which trapped Owen's hand, which was still tracing my spine in that Labrador-soothing way of his. I jerked forward. If I had to choose between a comfortable posture and Owen's hand on me, I'd sit up straight. I swept the useless notebook away from me. "Yeah. Fat lot of good it did me." I sighed, leaning into his caressing hand. "Is it a shifter thing? The touching?"

Owen's hand stalled, and I regretted the question. I didn't want him to stop. "I don't mind," I said, faster than I probably should have.

After a second he resumed his petting. "It's kind of a shifter thing, yeah. Most animals live in packs or prides, and while shifters don't have the same kind of dynamic, not as such, they still tend to stay in family groups. Touch and connection are pretty integral parts of shifter society."

"Even for owls?" Thanks to Animal Planet, I had a vague recollection that most owls were considered loners and didn't often live in groups. Though I also remembered that a group of owls was called a parliament, so groups or flocks weren't unheard-of concepts.

He smiled somewhat wistfully. "Shifter owls aren't quite as solitary as our native counterparts, though we're not quite as pack-oriented as some other avian species, and definitely not as much as the canines or even the felines." He shot me a knowing look. "I suspect any group things we rely on go to our human half rather than our owl half."

His hand stilled at the small of my back. "Does it bother you? I tend to be a bit more touchy-feely than other owls. I hang around enough shifters who aren't loners that I sometimes forget not everyone needs touch the same way."

"No. Don't stop... I mean, it's nice. It doesn't bother me." I arched my back a bit, a silent invitation to keep stroking me.

Owen didn't disappoint. If anything, his touch firmed. More pressure, less brushing of fingers. I closed my eyes, and eliminating one of my senses kicked the others into higher gear. The summer night sounds outside my window were clearer, a subtle symphony of crickets, rustling leaves, and distant coyotes that was uniquely Wyoming, uniquely beautiful. The pressure of Owen's touch took on new dimensions, feeling warmer, more important. Flavors I normally associated with Owen's scent settled on the back of my tongue. Snow and pine and the cool air of midnight all had a taste.

I don't know how long we sat like that. Eventually Owen's caresses slowed until they stopped altogether. He didn't lift his hand. It lingered, flexed. Goose bumps prickled along my skin, and I shivered.

There was something in the air, like a weighty expectation. I was afraid to open my eyes in case it broke the mood.

Owen cupped my face with the hand not planted at the small of my back. He swiped his thumb under one eye, along the cheekbone. Then, in a nearly identical motion, he traced his thumb along my eyebrow. I kept my lids sealed, and the brush of his skin across my eyelashes tickled enough to have my lips parting in a slight gasp. I nuzzled into his hand, both in a bid to increase the pressure and to return, at least in a small part, the caress. It was a very feline gesture, one I didn't want to think too hard about.

"Yusuf?" His breath ghosted along my cheek.

"Yeah, Owen?"

His combed his hand through my hair, tucking the almost-too-long strands of my bangs off my forehead. The hand planted at the small of my back lifted, and I pushed back, trying to prolong the contact. "Can you look at me?" With one hand palming my cheek, he used the other to tip my chin back.

Reluctantly, I blinked my eyes open.

The quick, easy smile I'd found so fascinating the first night I met him was missing. It had been replaced with something gentler, something more serious.

"I'd like to kiss you. Will you let me?"

Oh man. My heart throbbed, deep and almost sickeningly.

Owen. Owen wanted to kiss me. Kiss *me*. He hadn't asked the night before, which meant this was different somehow. More important, maybe. At least it felt that way.

I sucked in a breath. Licked my lips. Stared into those wide glowing amber eyes.

I wanted to say *yes* and *please* and *okay* and *right now*. But try as I might, the words wouldn't come. So I did the only thing I could do. I nodded.

This time his smile was sweet and full of joy. "Okay. Yeah."

He leaned up, and I held my breath.

His lips were soft, the stubble on his chin rough.

I didn't know what to do. Whether I should kiss him back or allow him free rein. At first his kiss was simple and sweet, a brush of lips against lips, nothing more. Then, when I didn't jerk back—or yank him to me—he pulled back long enough to gauge my interest. Last night had been quick, casual. This was anything but.

My eyes were wide, probably three sizes too big for my face. Even though I couldn't focus enough to see him well, I didn't close my eyes. His lips curled up, and I wanted to touch. To taste. I didn't wait for him to make the next move. I leaned forward, captured his mouth. I didn't know what I was doing. I didn't have a clue. But before I had time to worry about it, Owen took over. Oh, he wasn't forceful or demanding. He tilted his head, perfecting the fit of our lips. He tested. He teased. He tasted. And me, I reveled in each new touch, each new movement.

I was too caught up in everything he was doing so I could dissect the movements for future study. The first time he flicked at my bottom lip with the tip of his tongue, I shook. It tickled but didn't cause me to want to laugh. Instead, something twisted in my abdomen, a feeling both tantalizing and discomfiting. He didn't push. He didn't pressure for more. In fact, it was I who opened to him, drawing his tongue into my mouth.

I moaned.

He groaned.

I looped my arms around his neck, closing the distance between us. It was like someone or something activated a new facet in my brain. Or, more likely, my body. I needed to feel him, the hard lines of him against me. I needed to get closer, to touch as much of him as I could. I'm not even sure a complete melding of our bodies would be enough. I dug my fingers into his shirt, fisting the warm cotton.

Owen broke away, gasping for breath. He rested his forehead against mine, and I noticed that somewhere along the way I'd gone from sitting *next to* him on my bed to sitting *on* him on my bed. I straddled his lap, so between that and my extra few inches in height, I had to look down at him.

My body thrummed with excitement. I was also, I realized, hard. I wasn't embarrassed, not really, but my reaction, given everything else at this moment, seemed ill-timed. I leaned back, thinking I should probably not be climbing all over Owen like this. But then I noticed Owen was aroused too.

I scrambled off him. We were friends, weren't we? Sure, kissing like we had maybe stretched the bonds of friendship, but humping my friend was definitely crossing a line. Right? But maybe not. Not if he was as into it as he seemed.

I snatched a pillow from the top of my bed and covered my lap. I wanted to be smooth about it, but I'm pretty sure I came off as frantic and desperate.

Owen sat up straight, crossing one leg over the opposite knee, then stretching his arms out, a seemingly casual change of posture probably geared 100 percent to hiding his boner.

Damn, the whole thing was awkward, and Owen probably regretted the kiss. Especially if he hadn't intended it to go so far.

I cleared my throat. "So...."

Owen nodded. After a moment he patted his pockets before digging out his phone. A glance at the screen later, he said, "So, yeah. I should probably go. I've got to work the desk tonight."

"Right," I said.

"Right." After another awkward pause, he stood. "I guess I'll see you tomorrow."

"Sure."

He crossed to the door, opened it. He stilled, hand gripping the knob. "You want to do lunch tomorrow? We can meet after class."

I was a jittery mess, so my voice wasn't as calm as I'd hoped. "Yeah. That'd be great. Lunch."

As soon as the door closed behind him, I flung myself flat against my mattress and tried to smother myself with my pillow. "Argh." I tossed the pillow aside when I remembered breathing was actually a good thing. It had been one very strange day, and the last hour only made it worse.

Well, not worse. I ran my fingers across my lips. No, definitely not worse. Just… more complicated.

Chapter Ten

I HAD two phone calls the next day that indicated things were definitely more complicated.

The first call was from David. "Bad luck," he'd said while I was on my way to my first class. "Nothing's popped on my searches yet. Well, not nothing. Lots of results. But nothing connected to you." He was both quick and abrupt, giving the words a manic edge. Or an overcaffeinated one.

"How do you know that already?" He'd only agreed to help the day before.

"Ran the search overnight."

"Overnight? Did you sleep?"

"Nah. A little coffee, a couple energy drinks, and a bag of Doritos, and I'm good. I'll crash later today."

And here came the guilt. "No one expects you pull an all-nighter on this."

I heard the crisp *pop* of a soda can being opened. "This was the easy stuff. Didn't figure on getting the answers through a simple internet search. Had to eliminate the possibility ASAP. Needed to do it before digging into the next layers."

"So you're starting the next layers?" I was mildly curious about the steps one took to do the kind of algorithm-driven searches he was doing, but I recognized my computer and internet skills could be described as "adequate" at best, so even if he told me anything more specific than he had, I probably wouldn't have understood.

Several long swallows later, David said, "Yep. Layers."

He hung up a few seconds later, muttering something incomprehensible about data strings and search terms.

Almost immediately my phone rang again. The second conversation was with the receptionist at the campus medical center. Dr. Weyer apparently wanted to schedule a time to meet me. Reluctantly I agreed. In part because he was Owen's father, but also because he'd been right when he suggested it was a good idea to have a local doctor who was familiar with my history, especially one who understood the shifter aspects of my physiology.

As much as it made sense to see the doctor, he was Owen's father, which created a whole other string of reasons to be nervous. Mostly because of Owen. I just didn't want to come face-to-face with the father of the guy I'd fantasized about for the second night in a row. Last night, after I'd finally settled down enough to actually fall asleep, I'd woken up covered in sweat and jizz. I couldn't remember the last time I'd had a wet dream. I'd cleaned up as best I could, tossed the sticky sheets into the laundry basket, and fell back onto my comforter. My brain was filled with too much static—the make-out session, the erotic dream of which I could remember every single detail, how it felt when he touched me. Even his completely platonic touches. The worst part was the knowledge that I could walk down two flights of stairs and see him. Talk to him. He'd still be working his shift at the front desk.

So no, I didn't sleep.

And no, I didn't go see him.

I spent the entire night staring at my boring beige ceiling.

AFTER the three-hour wildlife conservation lecture, I exited the science building, having learned nothing new. Dr. Coleman gave me a concerned look after he dismissed the class, but I hustled out before he could corner me again. It wasn't like I could confess everything to him. Just because he taught at Cody College, and his boyfriend definitely skewed *other*, didn't mean it was completely safe to assume he was aware of the shifters among the population.

My phone vibrated in my pocket. I could go days without a phone call, and I'd already dealt with two this morning. And since my preclass calls hadn't exactly done anything to ease my anxiety, I was reluctant to answer this one.

The high-noon sun blazed from a clear Wyoming sky, so I had to tilt the phone to read the display when I pulled it out. Owen.

I considered—briefly—letting the call go to voicemail. Even though I was doing my best to perfect my avoidance skills, it seemed wrong somehow to practice on Owen.

"We're still on for lunch, right?" he asked as soon as I answered the call.

I looked at the time. "Yeah. It'll have to be a quick one, though. I've got an appointment with your dad at one."

The pause on the other end of the line went on long enough that I checked the phone to make sure we were still connected.

"Oh, cool," he finally said. "We should meet at the Union, then. It'll be quickest, and it's close to the medical center."

Something in his voice made me think maybe it wasn't cool, and I debated asking about it. But we were on the phone and would see each other in a minute. Maybe if I knew which part of his reply didn't ring true. Was he disappointed our time would be cut short? Was he worried about my health and the need to see a doctor? Did it mess with his plans?

"Okay," I said.

"Oh, I see you. Hanging up now."

I squinted against the sun, looking for Owen's form. I smelled him before I saw him. Winter snow, pine trees, and midnight. I'm not sure I would ever get used to it. A couple of seconds later, I swear I felt him approach behind me. I turned to face him.

If awkward could be a physical force, I'd have run into it. I didn't know what to say or what to do. I wanted to touch him, to hug him. I wanted to hide, worried he'd see remnants of last night's dream. What I ended up doing was forcing a completely fake smile on my face. "Hey, dude. How're things?" I immediately cringed. What the hell was that? I didn't say "dude," and "how're things" sounded like something one of my middle-aged doctors would have said when they wanted to sound approachable.

Owen peered at me. "That was the weirdest thing you've ever said around me."

I wilted. "Yeah. It was... weird." I didn't offer him any explanations, though. No need to make it even more awkward.

We started walking toward the Union. Our hands brushed. I jumped a foot to my right to avoid further contact. "Sorry."

"No biggie. I've always figured there was some kind of gravitational force between people. I tend to be pulled to people when I walk with them. I've had more than one person accuse me of wanting to hold their hands. Not that I think you think I want to hold your hand. Or not. Or that I do. I mean...."

I came to a halt at his babbling. "Wow. That's... wow."

He sucked in a deep breath. "You know what, ignore me. I'm totally making a fool of myself."

I couldn't stop the smile crossing my face. "Okay."

A few moments later, his hand brushed mine again. This time I didn't jump away.

Then he grabbed my hand, lacing our fingers together.

My heart sputtered in my chest. I shot him a look from the corner of my eye. I did not, however, pull my hand away.

"This is easier."

I licked my lips. "Okay."

"You don't mind?"

"No."

"Some people do. It's not 1950 anymore, but it's still Wyoming."

It took a second for the words to sink in. Holy shit. I was holding another man's hand, in public, in Wyoming.

Just because I hadn't seen any blatant signs of homophobia on campus didn't mean everyone was going to join the Love is Love brigade. I thought about Jonah and Owen's psych classmates and how open and accepting they'd been about Owen's sexuality and Dr. Coleman's scandalous affair with his TA. It had been the teacher-student part that had scandalized them, not the man-on-man part. I wasn't naïve enough to think all of Cody, Wyoming, or even all of Cody College would be as open, but if a large portion of the population could accept that people turn into animals, they could probably accept that some dudes were into dudes.

Besides, even if I didn't exactly know why Owen wanted to hold my hand, I enjoyed the contact too much to stop him.

I squeezed his hand. "Really. This is fine. It's more than fine. It's… nice."

The rest of the walk happened in silence.

We headed straight for the sandwich place after we entered the Union. Owen released my hand, but in the process he trailed his middle finger along my palm. Nerves fired up, sending jolts up my arm, through my chest, and straight to my groin. I bit my lip to keep from groaning and melting into a puddle of goo.

Unlike the first time I'd had lunch at the Union with Owen, I didn't second-guess my order. "Roast beef and cheddar, extra meat. Lettuce, tomatoes, pickles, black olives, and Italian vinaigrette."

I didn't have to look at Owen to know my order amused him. He huffed out a nearly silent laugh.

"And a bag of potato chips," I added.

He leaned toward me, bracing a hand on my shoulder and standing on his toes to whisper in my ear. "I'm teaching you well, aren't I?"

I shivered, trying not to think of the many things I figured he could teach me. Sandwiches were not on the list.

I shrugged, feigning nonchalance. "I can't deny you know your way around a sandwich. It helps I'm not constantly nauseated anymore."

Even the thought of it dimmed my enthusiasm. No, I wasn't feeling ill anymore, was I? And why not? Because apparently there was a lion inside me who wanted out. And the existence of the lion, outside the impossibility of shifters in general, meant my parents had been lying to me about something.

Owen squeezed my shoulder, massaging muscles that had grown tight. "It'll be fine. We'll figure it out."

I'd lost count over the years of how many times I'd heard some variation of that. I wished I didn't have fifteen years of failure to show me how unlikely it was.

We settled in at a four-top table in the corner, away from the smattering of other students throughout the dining hall. I took my time unwrapping my sandwich. I took my time inserting potato chips into the middle. I took my time because I didn't want to think about anything more complicated than my roast beef and cheddar sandwich, garnished with greasy, salty potato chips.

Owen had another Italian combo monstrosity and was equally deliberate in his potato chip placement. Maybe he was stalling too.

I couldn't stall too long, though. I had less than twenty minutes before I had to meet Dr. Weyer. I bit into my sandwich, taking a second to enjoy the combination of flavors.

"We should probably talk." Owen ignored his meal.

"Okay." I paused to pop a black olive slice into my mouth.

"I think we should visit your parents over the Fourth."

I inhaled roughly, which was stupid since I had a partially chewed olive in my mouth. Some piece of it went down the wrong way, my throat spasmed, and I choked. I coughed, so I knew I could breathe, but Owen's eyes widened. He darted around the table and whacked my back unnecessarily. When I stopped coughing long enough to speak, I asked, "You want to go to Chicago?"

He nodded, then immediately shook his head. "No. I mean, sure, I'd love to visit Chicago, but that's not why. I talked to David this morning, and I've been thinking."

"Yeah, he called me too."

"Right." Owen picked up a potato chip and started crumbling little pieces off the edges. "So you know he didn't find anything in the open adoption records."

"Right. Which could mean I'm not adopted." I was determined to be positive.

"Or it could mean your adoption was closed, or sealed, whatever the word is."

I shrugged. He wasn't wrong, but I preferred my answer.

"It's going to take him a little longer to delve into the sealed records."

"I've got time," I said. There was no deadline, no ticking clock.

"But it's hurting you."

"Hurting me?"

"Yeah," he said. "Hurting you here." He tapped at his chest. "The stress and uncertainty aren't good for you."

I didn't know if that was the sweetest thing someone had ever said to me or the most condescending. "I can handle it."

"Yeah, but you shouldn't have to." He reached out, covered my hand with his. "You haven't been sleeping. You're losing weight again. It's not good for you."

I crossed one arm defensively over my chest. I didn't pull away from his hold on my other hand, though. I couldn't quite make myself sever the connection. "The thing is, I've been dealing with this kind of stuff my whole life. I may be battling insomnia or stress, but I'm healthier than I have been in years. Maybe ever."

"Wouldn't it be better to get your answers? Just because you can deal with it doesn't mean you should have to."

"But what if the answers are worse than not knowing? For real, Owen. I don't know if I can handle the answers if it means my parents have been lying to me my whole life."

His face softened, earnestness pouring off him in waves. "I'm not sure there's an answer that doesn't mean they've been lying. Either you're adopted and they lied to you about it, or one or the both of them are shifters and they've been lying about that."

"Yeah. And I don't know which would be the better option. Both suck."

"You avoiding the question doesn't change the truth of the answer. I think…." He paused, biting his lip for a second before continuing. "I think part of you is hoping for another option, one in which your parents are biologically your parents and they are not shifters. I'm not sure that hope is good for you. Not if it means you're burying your head in the sand."

"Are you headshrinking me? Like a project for your class?"

He tightened his fingers around mine. "No, Yusuf. I just want what's best for you."

At that, I did pull away. "You know what? People have been smothering me, making decisions for me, my whole life, all because they wanted what's best for me. You know what they didn't do? They didn't ask me what I wanted. They didn't let me decide what's best for me. I know my parents did it out of love, doctors did it to solve a puzzle or to fulfill a sacred calling, or whatever. I don't get why you're doing it."

He opened his mouth, then snapped it shut almost immediately.

I folded the paper wrap back around my sandwich. I shoved it and my half-empty bag of chips into my shoulder bag and stood. "I've got to go. I've got an appointment. One where someone with undoubtedly good intentions is going to tell me what to do for my own good."

I turned away, took a step, stopped. I didn't look back when I said, "You're my friend, Owen, and I appreciate that you care enough to want to help. But I get enough pressure from everyone else in my life. I don't need more."

Chapter Eleven

FIVE minutes later I sat in the small waiting room in the campus medical center, curled into myself, wishing for something solid to bang my head against.

I'd overreacted. Seriously. I hadn't been wrong, not really, but I couldn't believe I'd said that to Owen. To Owen. My first friend. They guy who'd kissed me last night. Kissed me like he'd meant it and like I was special. I felt kind of the same way as when I'd fought with my parents about stopping the medical research and therapies so I could go to college. They hadn't objected because I wanted an education. But I'd been doing classes online, so why couldn't I continue that way? Why did I have to leave? I needed to stay where Dr. Mirza was, where there were people who could help when things worsened. And if I had to go to school, why did I have to go so far away? Every question was a pinprick of blame, of responsibility, expertly applied, until it felt like the guilt of it all was going to overwhelm me.

Owen wasn't my parents. I didn't owe him anything. But the shame felt the same.

I wasn't like Owen. I didn't have an avalanche of words at my beck and call. Sure, they were there in my head, but it was hard for me to give them voice, especially when they mattered. I needed to talk to Owen, to explain. Maybe to apologize.

I grabbed my phone from my pocket, pulled up Owen's name on my contact list, then hesitated. I should call him. I didn't know a lot about interpersonal relationships, but I knew that text apologies were lame.

"Mr. Franke?" The lady behind the medical center's registration desk waved to me.

I hit the icon to send a text. I kept one eye on where I was going and the other on my phone as I typed. *Sorry. Will talk soon, OK?* I hit Send and tossed the phone in my shoulder bag instead of returning it to my pocket. If he texted back while I was talking with his father, I didn't think I could keep myself from looking at the message. Better all around if I didn't know when—if— he responded.

The nurse took me to a small office instead of an exam room. I relaxed a little. Dr. Weyer looked up from behind his desk when I entered with the receptionist. "Have a seat."

The receptionist closed the door behind me. Normally it wouldn't have even registered, but after everything with Owen over the last twenty-four hours, it felt a little ominous sitting in front of Owen's dad.

Up close with Dr. Weyer, and now that my brain wasn't reeling from discovering that not only did shifters exist but I was one, I realized he was older than I'd have expected. He had to be well into his sixties, which meant he'd have been in his forties when Owen was born. It wasn't unusual, I guess, but since my own parents hadn't yet hit fifty, it seemed like a huge age gap. Maybe it was the reason Owen said he and his parents weren't as close as me and mine.

"I'm glad you were able to come in this morning," Dr. Weyer said, folding his hands on his desk. His whole office was pretty generic, but I supposed it was shared between all the doctors on staff. There'd been no name plate on the door, only a sign stating "Physicians." There were no name tags or personal photos. Just a computer monitor, a keyboard, and a little stand with an assortment of business cards.

I nodded. "No problem."

"As I said this morning, I reviewed your medical records. You've been through a lot, haven't you?"

It was clearly a rhetorical question, so I didn't answer it. I just shrugged.

"It's unfortunate you didn't have a shifter doctor," he said. "It would have saved you a lot of uncomfortable procedures and tests. Of course, if you'd had a shifter doctor, you wouldn't have needed to see a doctor in the first place."

"Excuse me?"

"Joey, there was nothing medically wrong with you."

I sat up straight. "Excuse me? Something was absolutely wrong with me." There was no way the pain, the rashes, the fevers, the aches, the vomiting, any of it, didn't happen. "I'm not a hypochondriac, I don't have Munchausen. My parents don't have hypochondria or Munchausen Syndrome by Proxy." We'd heard it all, and it had always been ruled out in the end.

"I believe you. That's not what I meant."

Since he seemed genuine, I settled back in my chair.

"You're a shifter," he said.

"Right. Asiatic lion by the sound of it."

"That's what Owen tells me. But you were unaware of it until a few weeks ago."

"That's right."

"I've made some inquiries and found a handful of individuals who have reported the same symptoms you had growing up."

Hope kindled in my chest. I'd been there before; I knew better than to trust that finally I had an answer. "Yeah?"

"It's happened with individuals whose shifter gene is dormant."

"How, dormant? Like, could I be only a quarter shifter or something?" Maybe this was it. Maybe this was the answer to why I was a shifter and neither of my parents were. Maybe it was a recessive gene. Maybe they hadn't lied to me my entire life. Stupid maybes were as bad as hope, but just as hard for me to deny.

"It's not a matter of percentages, not really. It's not really even a dominant or recessive gene. The shifter gene doesn't present itself at all unless at least one of the young's parents is fully shifter. Even two individuals who are each half shifter will not have shifter children."

I deflated. Should have known better than to hope. "So what you're saying is at least one of my parents is one hundred percent shifter, but that for some reason, the gene in me stayed dormant my whole life."

"Correct."

"Why was it dormant? And why did I suddenly turn into an Asiatic lion?"

"In the other reported cases, it was a matter of proximity. Children who grew up away from shifter communities for one reason or another. While they were separated from other shifters—and we're talking long-term separation here, not vacations or what have you—they were ill, but when they began spending time among other shifters, especially in large groups, they changed into their animal form for the first time. And the symptoms, their previous illnesses, went away."

"Why symptoms in the first place, though?"

Dr. Weyer sighed. "Based on the handful of instances we have records for, the best we can tell is that not shifting was necessary to keep the individual safe. It's like a biological protection. But it's also unnatural. Basically, the individuals' bodies were fighting themselves. Both needing to hide and needing to protect themselves."

I snorted. "It sounds like I had some kind of autoimmune issue after all. Dr. Mirza would be happy to know he wasn't far off."

He cocked his head, and the resemblance to both Owen and an owl was stronger than ever.

"Well, it's like an extreme autoimmune reaction, right? My body was literally fighting itself."

Dr. Weyer smiled, and this time it was more genuine and less perfunctory. "That's certainly one way to look at it."

"And I turned into a lion because now I'm around other shifters?"

"Exactly. Then the full moon triggered your first shift."

A new kernel of hope, along with a smidgeon of hurt, bloomed in me. "So that means neither of my parents is a shifter? I have to be adopted?"

He grimaced a little. "Not exactly. Some animals—and therefore the shifters who change into those animals—are closely tied to a pack structure. Wolves, for example, are notoriously pack-centric. They need to be around other shifters, and usually in larger groups. The more pack-oriented the shifter's other form, the more direct contact with shifters they need."

"Which means what in terms of me?"

"You are a felid—specifically a lion—shifter. Lions are as pack-centric as wolves. Which means you need more contact with shifters than some. If only one of your parents is a shifter, it's likely there would not be enough shifter contact for your shifter side to express itself."

"Which means we still don't know for sure if my parents have lied about what they are or whether I'm adopted."

"No, I'm sorry." He leaned forward, resting his arms on the empty surface of the desk. "That being said, I am confident now that your shifter side has finally emerged, you will no longer suffer any of the symptoms or illnesses you grew up with. For all intents and purposes, you are healthy and should be able to live a normal life."

"Normal except for the part where I turn into a lion."

"Well, that's true. I would like to see you gain some weight and get some sleep. As a shifter, your metabolism is greatly enhanced, and you'll need to double, if not triple, your previous caloric intake. You need to increase your protein for sure. You're underweight, which is dangerous to others."

"Dangerous?"

"Imagine a hungry lion prowling through campus. The hungrier the animal, the less control they have. Which means you might decide a drunken frat boy looks like the perfect midnight snack."

I rested my hand over my suddenly queasy stomach. I was glad my sandwich from lunch was still in my bag rather than in my gut.

He noticed my reaction. "No need to panic. Eat more, gain some weight, you'll be fine. That being said, you'll want to do all of your shifting for a while in the presence of other shifters. For the safety of everyone, it's best if you do the full moon hunts with other large predators—the bears or the wolves—until you've learned control."

"What if I don't shift at all? I don't want to risk hurting anyone."

He shook his head. "Now that you've shifted, you won't be able to stop yourself from doing it again. And the more you shift, the more control you'll have. You'll shift at the full moon in two weeks whether you want to or not. Eventually you'll be able to decide you only want to shift once a month, but until then, you need a mentor. Someone to work with you until you can shift when and where you want to. Right now, you're a risk. All it will take is getting angry or scared enough, and the shift will come. You need to know how to keep it from happening and to identify the triggers."

Kind of like at Buddy's Café yesterday, when I was tempted to fang out in jealousy over the oh-so-perfect David. I didn't imagine an Asiatic lion rampaging through a café would be a good thing. "Um, yeah. That sounds like a good idea."

"Someone from the local council will get in touch. They're probably going to set up a formal mentorship with the bears. Buddy and his family are strong enough to keep your lion in line, but laid-back enough they won't look at you as a dominance challenge."

"No. Definitely don't want to challenge the bears to a dominance fight," I said weakly.

Damn. Was this my life now? Dominance fights with bears and snacking on frat boys?

OWEN waited for me outside the medical center. He leaned against the pale brick wall, hands tucked into his cargo shorts pockets. The sun, still bright in the afternoon sky, glinted off his ash-blond hair. He looked good in sunlight, but he looked better at night, when the dark outside and the pale glow of the moon showcased his eyes in all their glory.

"Hey," I said.

"Hey." He hunched into his shoulders a bit, looking as uncomfortable as I'd ever seen him. I really didn't like seeing him that way.

I had a thought. "Aren't you supposed to be in class right now?"

He shrugged. "I didn't want to wait to talk to you."

I pointed over my shoulder. "Your father is right in there. I'm not sure he'd approve of you skipping class."

"He'll deal. Unless I royally screw up and fail the class, which I won't, he won't care."

I leaned against the wall next to him, tucking my hands in my pockets, mirroring his pose.

"I'm sorry. I didn't mean to push," he said.

"No, I'm sorry. I overreacted."

We stood there a while, neither speaking. I stared out to the line of mountains in the distance. "I don't know if I'll ever get used to that," I said, nodding my chin toward the ridgeline. "I mean, the Chicago skyline is pretty iconic, but there's something about the mountains. The rough-around-the-edges beauty. It's not tame. It's not flashy. It's something to be respected. Someday I'm going to get closer. Do some hiking. Or maybe camping. I want to be able to say I was there."

"We can make that happen. Either hiking or camping. Or both. I've got camping gear. But if you've never done it, it's something you'll want to work your way up to."

"Someday," I agreed. It was nice having a someday. For a long time, I didn't want to plan too far ahead. I didn't know when or if my illness would take a turn for the worse. When I was having a particularly good week, I was happy to be able to watch a movie from my couch, pain-free, with no need for special equipment. Now I was talking about hiking and camping in the mountains like it was a real possibility. Because, for the first time, it actually was.

I turned to Owen. "Do you really think going to Chicago will be useful?"

"Yeah. Right now we've got too many possibilities and not enough answers. With every answer we find, we can narrow the list of possibilities."

"What do you think we can discover in Chicago that David can't find through his hacking skills?"

"David is focusing on the adoption side, right?"

"Right."

"Well, if you aren't adopted, then one of your parents is a shifter. And since you don't want to ask"—I was relieved he said it without any judgment or pressure— "the next best way to discover if one of them is a shifter is for a shifter to meet them. I knew you were a shifter the moment we met."

"You did?"

"Sure. There are things that stand out, if you know what you're looking for."

I distantly remember the conversation he'd had with Cocky Boy and Anxious Girl. "Tapetum lucidum."

"That's one way. There's an energy, too, kind of a like an aura. A vibe other shifters can pick up. Or a scent."

Now that he mentioned it, I realized I'd been able to pick up on signs. I'd known David was a shifter, for example. And there were a couple of others I'd run across on campus. "Do you think I'd be able to figure it out when I'm home? So you don't have to come all that way."

His face fell. "Oh, well, maybe. If you don't want me to go along, we could do some tests. Teach you some of the signs."

"It's not that I don't want you to go along." I couldn't handle the disappointment in his voice and posture. He looked rejected. "But flights out of Wyoming aren't cheap, and it's a lot to ask of someone."

"Is that the only reason? Because I want to be there for you, but not if it's an inconvenience, or if it makes you uncomfortable. Definitely not if you don't want me to be there."

Did I want him to go along? I took a second to think about it. Yes, yes, I did. The idea of seeing my parents again with all these questions taking up more than their share of real estate in my brain made me nervous. Who knew what I would say or do if I had to face them one-on-one? I'd probably do my best to avoid the whole conversation altogether and pretend all was right in my world. Having someone there to act as backup, someone who'd both have my back and keep me on mission, would be nothing but a benefit. But it seemed like a lot to ask of a new friend.

"It'd be nice having you there," I finally admitted. "But logistically—"

He waved that aside. "If logistics is the only obstacle, we're good."

I wavered. "At least let me get the airfare." I hadn't been kidding when I mentioned the cost of flights to and from Wyoming. A downside to not having a major airline hub located nearby, probably.

"You don't need to worry about it. Really. My parents have so many frequent flyer miles stocked up, we could probably circle the globe and not have to pay a dime."

"Seriously?"

"Yeah. Mom travels a lot for work." He grinned. "Tell you what, if you spring for some of this famous Chicago-style pizza I've heard so much about, we'll call it even."

Lou Malnati's was a small price to pay for moral support and answers.

Chapter Twelve

LESS than a week later, I boarded a plane bound for Chicago, by way of Denver, with Owen.

I hadn't seen him much over the last few days. Except at night. I still wandered down his way during his shifts at the front desk at Matthison Hall. Sometimes we played chess. Sometimes we worked on homework. Thanks to the Fourth of July holiday, we got an extended weekend from class. Mostly this meant we had a great excuse to go visit my parents. I hated that I had to make an excuse. They were ecstatic. The only hiccup had been when I mentioned I'd invited Owen along.

"I know we don't have a guest room anymore." We'd lost the extra space when my parents downsized to help pay my medical bills. "But Owen is cool crashing on the couch." I don't know that anyone had ever slept on the couch before. At least not outside of dozing off during the nightly news. And we'd never invited anyone to stay the night, let alone for a long weekend. Not ever.

"Is it safe? With your immune—"

"I'm doing so much better now," I rushed to reassure her.

It wasn't fair of me to basically present my mom and dad with a done deal, but that's what I did. I may have insinuated that if Owen wasn't welcome, I wasn't going to come. At which point Mom stopped objecting, but I could practically hear the worry in her tense silence.

I'd waited until we were seated on the twenty-seven-passenger jet headed to Denver before I broached the subject of my apparent health with Owen. "My parents can't know I'm healthy."

He looked up from the seat belt he'd been locking into place. "Huh?"

I fiddled with the magazine pocket in front of me rather than meet his eyes. "I've been sick as long as I can remember. Ever since *that night*"—which is how I referred to the night three weeks ago when my inner Asiatic lion decided to break out—"I've been healthier than I've ever been. I'm not sick anymore. Not at all. They're going to be suspicious."

"So you're going to, what, fake being sick?"

I glanced at him from the corner of my eye. I couldn't read his voice, so I needed to catch his expression. It wasn't disapproval, at least. Or shock. He looked confused. "I don't know what else to do. I mean, I need to seem okay enough they don't steal my ID so I can't get an a plane and then wrap me up and ship me off to Dr.

Mirza, but not so good they question why I've suddenly got more energy or strength than ever before."

"Steal your ID?" Owen chuckled. "That's randomly specific. Is it something they've threatened to do in the past?"

Heat rushed up my neck. "Well, no, but if they truly thought I was at risk, they'd find a way to hustle me in to see Dr. Mirza."

"And they didn't make a fuss about the move across the country? They just let you go?"

"They didn't let me go so much as they resigned themselves to the fact that I was going to do it, with or without their permission." I closed my eyes for a moment, thinking back. "I was tired. They were so determined to figure out what was wrong, to find the cure, because they didn't want to lose me. Not without a fight. And I was tired of fighting. After so many disappointments, so many trials without the slightest sign of improvement, I was tired of it. In the end I decided it would be better to find a way to live with the symptoms than to keep searching for answers that didn't exist. It was partly for them too. With every new test, every new theory, they would convince themselves that this time it would work, that this time they'd find the answers they were looking for. And every time, when it didn't work and they didn't get the answers, it killed something in them. I didn't want them to have to keep riding that roller coaster of high hopes and bitter disappointments."

Owen had turned to face me as fully as his seat belt would allow. "For someone who doesn't talk much, sometimes you make up for it."

I shrugged, suddenly uncomfortable. "It's why I don't think either of them could be a shifter. If there is any chance they knew about that side of me, that there was even a chance the shifter gene was causing some sort of extreme autoimmune reaction, they'd have done something about it, found other shifters to hang around, something. There's no way they'd have let me go through that—or put themselves through that—otherwise."

Some weird feeling, kind of like anxiety mixed with mourning and resentment, curled around me. I couldn't believe they were secret shifters. But that only left a secret adoption. And the idea of that was nearly enough to break my heart. Which was why I desperately wanted there to be some other explanation. Anything that didn't mean my parents had been lying to me all this time.

I don't think I'd ever get used to the small planes used by some of the regional airports. The twenty-seven-seater jet that took us over the mountains from Cody to Denver reminded me of a survival book I'd read when I was twelve. I couldn't help but look around to find out, should we crash, where the tools, the spare food, the luggage, etc. was located. Because if the plane crashed while passing over the Rockies, of course I would survive. I even looked around to see who the most vulnerable were so I'd know who to help first.

Without thinking, I mentioned this to Owen, who laughed. "I had no idea you had such a hero complex."

I grunted, crossing my arms over my chest. "At least if the plane starts to go down, you can shift and fly away. The rest of us will have to make do with—" I peered into the pocket in front of me. "—a bag of mini pretzels, a magazine from 2012, and a condom. Seriously?" I pulled the square out and examined the label.

Owen's grin was blinding. "You've heard of the mile-high club, right?"

"But in this plane? How would that even work?" Not that I'd ever figured out how people made it work on the bigger aircrafts. "There's barely room for one regular-sized person in the bathroom, let alone two people." I twisted my shoulders, trying to imagine the contorting that would be required.

This time Owen's laugh drew attention from the flight attendant—the smaller plane only had the one—who was strapped into her seat at the front of the cabin. She did a quick scan to make sure we weren't unruly or panicking or whatever they worried about on these flights.

"I can honestly say I've never thought about it too closely before." Then he leered at me in an exaggerated fashion. "Wanna find out?" He waggled his eyebrows at me.

I knew he was kidding. I knew he didn't mean it, but my face burned and all the saliva in my mouth dried up at the thought. No, the dirty dreams I'd been having of Owen had not stopped over the last week. In fact they were escalating, if anything. Tired of waking up hard and flustered, I'd done what every other normal, healthy, red-blooded man would do. I explored internet porn and masturbated. And immediately cleared my browser history each and every time.

"Oh my! What is that look about?"

I cleared my throat. Then, before I could confess any of my wildly inappropriate thoughts, I tore into the pretzel bag and poured half the contents into my mouth. I choked, because dry mouth and pretzels were a bad combination. Owen patted my back oh so helpfully, chuckling the whole time while I wheezed and attempted to cough pretzel dust out of my esophagus.

"Now I really need to know what's going through your head."

I dug into my backpack, which was stored under the seat in front of me, and pulled out a bottle of water I'd picked up in one of the airport shops. It helped with the choking but did nothing to cool my thoughts.

"We're going to talk about something else and pretend this didn't happen," I told him when I could talk again. I regretted the words as soon as said them. My comments only reinforced the awkwardness of it all.

"Sure. If that's what you want." He smirked, and then he patted my thigh, and I about burst out of my seat.

"How long is this flight again?"

His gaze lingered for a moment, considering me. I wanted desperately to know what he was thinking, while at the same time I was grateful I couldn't read his mind. He couldn't have known exactly where my mind went, but it seemed like he had a good idea. Thankfully he accepted my change of subject. "We've got about an hour left."

I searched for something safer to talk about. "I love how the land looks from up here, especially when you can see the jagged edges and shadows of the mountains. It looks harsh and imposing from the sky, but softer somehow from the ground."

"I don't really like flying in planes," he said.

"No?"

"I think it's a control thing. Like, when I'm flying"— the subtle emphasis he put on the word told me he didn't mean traveling by plane, but meant flying in his shifted form—"I can gauge the change in wind currents. I control my speed and ascent. In a plane, I have to trust someone else. And it's kind of claustrophobic, you know? The space is close, and there's no room to move around."

"How often do you shift and fly? Clearly there's a pull at the full moon, but you can do it other times?"

"Yeah. Shifters can generally shift whenever they want. Most, outside of some individuals who have amazing powers of control and experience, have to change at the full moon. How often shifters change outside of the moon depends on what they're used to and what they need."

"Meaning?"

"Well, some people who have high-stress jobs shift more often as a way to release some of the pressure. Some people who live and work closer to bigger cities may have to go longer between shifts so they don't risk discovery. There are some, who have almost always been around other shifters, who change a lot, because they never learned the control not to shift whenever they get upset, or they never saw the need not to shift when they wanted to. Kind of depends."

"How often do you shift?"

He shrugged. "About once a week, at least. As an owl, I'm pretty comfortable in the night and in the dark, so I don't have to worry about being seen. Unlike you," he said, nudging me with his shoulder. "A great horned owl in Wyoming at night is no big deal. If anyone sees you wandering around, in the day or at night, people are going to freak. Next thing you know, you'll be picked up by some big-cat rescue operation."

"How often do you think I should shift?"

"What did my dad say?"

"He didn't mention it."

"How about whoever has been helping you work on control?"

I squinted at him. "Huh?"

"Someone is working with you, right?"

"Your father mentioned something about reaching out to some bears, but beyond that, I haven't heard anything."

Owen clenched his fists. "Yusuf, when was the last time you shifted?"

"What do you mean? I haven't shifted since that night."

He closed his eyes. "Damn it."

"What?"

"Someone should have been working with you over the last few weeks."

"Your dad only mentioned it a few days ago."

"I can't believe I didn't think about it sooner. Dad probably wanted to make sure he had his answers before talking with you. And he probably didn't want to set up something before he spoke to you. It's just like him." Owen banged his head against his seat back. "This could be a serious problem. He should have warned you, or at least warned me. I'm not the ideal mentor for you, but we could have been working out some of it."

"Is it really that big of a deal? I mean, I haven't been sick. I haven't accidentally shifted. I'm eating more protein. I'm actually starting to put on a little weight." I tugged at the T-shirt I wore to illustrate the way it clung a little tighter to my chest.

"How many times have you felt like you might shift?"

I shook my head, confused.

"Remember the day at Buddy's with David? You were on the edge then, right?"

"But I didn't shift, so that's good, right? Maybe I don't need to shift the way others do. I have to admit, it freaked me out. I wouldn't be upset if it didn't happen again."

Owen rubbed his forehead. "The thing is, it's going to happen again. At the very least, it's going to happen at full moons. But if you can't control it, or if the feral half overrides your human half, you could hurt yourself. Or hurt someone else."

Chills skittered down my spine. "That's unnerving. I guess I better call your dad or someone about the bears."

"You said my dad mentioned the bears. So he wants you to work with the Bradys."

"The Bradys?"

"There are other bear clans but only one clan of grizzlies. No one else would be big enough to stop you if things went wrong. You remember Buddy? He's the oldest Brady son. And you met Jonah; he's Buddy's youngest brother. There are a couple other sons, but I don't know where they are. I think Jimmy might be in California, and I haven't heard anything about Trace in a while."

This was all very fascinating, but except for Buddy and Jonah, these were just names without context. "I still don't know what that means for me. I mean, maybe the Brady brothers don't want to be my mentors."

"Well, with Jimmy and Trace gone, that leaves only Buddy and Jonah. And, I'll be honest, Jonah's a great guy, but he's not mature or experienced enough to give you the guidance you need. Which leaves Buddy. That's unfortunate."

"What's wrong with Buddy? He seemed okay that night you tranqed me."

"Buddy is an odd guy. He's kind of a recluse, actually. He owns the café but is rarely seen there. And he tends to disappear for weeks at a time, without telling anyone where he's at. After his parents died, he raised his younger brothers, but as soon as Jonah got old enough to take care of himself, he sort of dropped off the face of the earth. I was surprised Dad found him that night, to be honest. Which is why," Owen said on a drawn-out sigh, "you probably haven't heard from him yet. He's hard to reach at the best of times. Dad's probably left him messages, but who knows if Buddy's even seen them yet."

"And if we don't hear from Buddy? What does that mean?"

"I'm not sure. The council will probably have to get involved, find another lion shifter, maybe. But then you'd probably have to go to them."

"Go to them? They'd make me move? Can they do that?"

"The council is pretty hands-off, but there are some things they can enforce. If you pose a risk, either to other shifters, humans, or even the risk of exposure, they're going to do whatever they need to do to prevent it from happening. If you go feral…."

I remembered what Dr. Weyer had said that first night. "Yeah. Feral shifters get put down."

"It won't come to that. When we get back, we'll track down Buddy." Owen stretched his neck, arching it from side to side. Vertebrae popped. "I guess it doesn't matter much now, but we'll have to push harder when we get back to campus. There's no time to put it off anymore. The next full moon is only a few days after we get back to Cody."

The pilot announced that we were preparing for the descent into Denver. I closed my eyes and leaned back. Owen had given me a lot to think about.

Chapter Thirteen

SEVERAL hours and a stopover in Denver later our plane taxied into O'Hare International Airport. The minute we were given leave to, Owen stood. He'd been getting twitchier with each passing hour. When the passengers in front of us had disembarked, I ducked out of my seat. I pulled out my cell phone and turned off airplane mode. "I'm going to let my parents know we've landed. Find out how soon they'll be up front."

We'd barely stepped through the gate when my phone blew up. I'd missed eight calls and had twenty texts. "What the hell?"

Owen was looking at his own phone, cursing. I peeked over at it and saw he'd missed as many calls and had twice as many texts.

The texts were all from David, each one more urgent than the next.

Search results complete. No adoption records in US
Started intl search
Where are you? Need to talk
Srsly. Need to talk ASAP
Call me!!!
URGENT!
THIS IS FUCKING SERIOUS!

The last thirteen texts were all sent with exactly five minutes between each one. They all said *CALL ME!! URGENT!!*

Owen flashed his screen at me, showing a list of messages that were pretty much the same as mine.

I didn't bother to listen to the voicemail message. It would likely be more of the same. Even while I watched, another text came up, but this one was from my parents.

In baggage claim area. See you there.

I sent a thumbs-up sign to my parents' text before shoving my phone into my pockets.

We'd carried on our luggage, but I nodded to the signs pointing us to baggage claim and my parents. "Please tell me David is the type to be dramatic and hysterical with little provocation." I slung my duffel bag over my shoulder. Owen copied the motion with his own backpack.

"Nope. He's easily excitable, but not the type to panic. And this is total panic."

"What the hell could have happened to cause this?"

"I've got no idea." Owen tapped at his screen. We waited through six rings before David's voice came through, telling them to leave a message.

We exchanged nervous looks; then Owen said, "We'll try again when we reach your place. He's waited this long, so I guess he can wait another hour."

I wasn't thrilled to put it off, not after the extreme texts, but if David didn't answer his phone, what were our options? Feeling more than a little anxious, we made our way toward baggage claim.

At the first sight of my parents, I forgot the underhanded reasons for our visit and the niggly worry over David's texts. I was so damned happy to see them, I shoved my bag at Owen and barreled toward them. I flung my arms around my mom, squeezing her tight. She was soft and warm and smelled like home. Growing up, there'd been no artificial scents, no flowers, no exotic spices. Everything had been sterilized and hypoallergenic. Even her soaps and shampoos. But here, with my newly augmented olfactory ability, I caught an underlying aroma of rosewood and daffodils I suspected was inherent to her.

She didn't, however, smell at all animallike. With Owen and Buddy, and even David in the coffee shop, there'd been a hint of something wild.

She jerked in my embrace. Hugging was not something we'd done much of. Not because of any lack of desire on my parents' part, I realized, but because they'd had to be careful. Touch without proper protective gear could be dangerous for someone whose immune system was compromised. Or so they'd been told. Once the surprise cleared, she wrapped her arms around me too.

"I missed you," I murmured, giving her one last squeeze. "I hadn't realized how much until now." Maybe it was the time spent with Owen. Touch, whether hugging or brushing shoulders or even holding hands, was a big part of Owen and his friends' daily lives. I'd started seeing it as normal and acceptable.

She was barely five feet tall, so she had to reach up to pat my cheeks. She spoke softly in Persian, then said in English, "Look at you. You look... well. Better."

I remembered I had to play it up a little. Better was fine, but I couldn't be drastically, miraculously cured. "I'm doing all right in Wyoming. Maybe it's the mountain air."

"It looks good on you," she said, giving my cheek one last tap before stepping aside to let my dad greet me.

He stood there awkwardly for a moment. He wasn't very tall—shorter than me by a few inches—and he had the dark blond hair and blue eyes of his German ancestors. We did the embarrassing shuffle where we each brought up one hand, then the other, then stepped forward and backward, as though we didn't know whether to shake hands or hug. My height may not have come from him, but clearly the socially awkward gene hadn't missed me. "Hi, Dad."

He ruffled my hair like he'd done when I was little, and it made something tighten in my throat. This was my father. I didn't smell anything to indicate shifter, and I didn't see the reflected light in his eyes indicating tapetum lucidum. I swallowed past the lump disappointment left in my throat.

Owen moved up next to me, both our bags looped over his shoulders.

I needed to make introductions. I could do this. Introduce my parents to a friend. A friend whose kisses turned me inside out. A friend who was there to help me prove—or disprove—that my parents had been lying to me my whole life.

"Mom, Dad, this is my friend Owen Weyer. Owen, meet my parents, Joseph and Amaya Franke." The whole thing sounded ridiculously formal. I'd never really had to do an introduction like this before. My palms were sweaty, and I didn't know what to do with my hands.

Owen grinned broadly and shook my dad's hand with the same natural enthusiasm he did everything else. "It's so great to meet you. Yusuf has told me so much about you. It's great to finally meet you in person."

Mom arched her brows at his use of my given name.

"Is this all you brought?" Dad asked, nodding to the luggage.

"Yeah, since we're only going to be here a couple of days, we didn't need much." I took my bag from Owen. I couldn't believe I'd shoved it at him like that.

"You must be hungry after such a long day," Mom said.

My stomach immediately growled, despite the big lunch I'd had in Denver while we waited for our connecting flight to Chicago.

"I have baked chicken breasts, brown rice, and steamed vegetables."

Inwardly I cringed. It was the kind of healthy meal I'd spent my life eating, at least outside of the times I'd been put on one particular diet plan or another. "I promised Owen I'd take him Lou Malnati's. Show him authentic Chicago-style pizza."

Both of my parents stopped in their tracks. "You can't—" Dad started.

"You shouldn't—" Mom began at the same time.

I sighed. Deep-dish pizza was not something I would eaten before moving to Wyoming. It wasn't something I *could* eat before Wyoming. But, damn it, I was old enough to make my own dinner choices.

My parents looked at each other, holding some kind of silent communication.

Owen placed his hand on my wrist. "It's okay. I like chicken."

My parents' silent conversation halted as they both focused on Owen's hand on me.

I sighed. "Fine. But tomorrow we'll go to Lou's."

WHEN we reached the condo, I dragged Owen to my room. I said something about it being a chance for him to "freshen up," whatever the hell that meant, so my parents wouldn't question it. Really it was an excuse to get away from my parents, who'd spent the entire car ride from the airport in excruciating silence. It wasn't all about escape, though. We needed to reach David.

I'd forgotten how barren my room was. Four walls, a full-size bed, and a nightstand. The chest of drawers was kept in my closet because it was one more thing that could gather dust and germs. Owen didn't seem bothered by the Spartan chamber and hadn't given the industrial-sized air purifier a second glance. If he wasn't going to mention it, I certainly wasn't going to get worked up over it.

Owen sat cross-legged on my bed, back facing the wall. I sat next to him. My laptop was between us, David's face filling the monitor. He didn't look quite as perfect as he had the day we met. Dark circles shadowed his eyes, and his lips were pale. His slightly too long hair stood out in several directions.

"What the hell did you get me involved in?" he demanded the minute the Skype call connected. "If you've landed me on some international terrorist watch list, I'm going to be pissed."

I gasped. "International terrorist—"

"What happened?" Owen asked.

"I got cocky, that's what happened. And I triggered a freaking honeypot."

I blinked at the screen. "I don't know what that means. But I take it it's bad?"

David ran a hand through his rumpled hair. "It's a trap meant to lure hackers, one that allows police, or whichever officials are interested, to get data on hackers. I shouldn't have missed it, but they'd hidden it well. And who'd hide a fucking honeypot that way? I mean, the whole point is to make it an easy, obvious target to tempt hackers, not bury it under so much code someone would only run across it by accident."

Owen leaned into the computer. "Before you get too caught up in who's responsible, why don't you start from the beginning and explain what happened."

"Fine. This morning I barricaded myself in my bedroom while the rest of my family did holiday weekend stuff. I had to pretend that I didn't feel good, and since shifters are rarely ill, half my family is convinced I've developed some kind of freakish disease, and the other half thinks I'm 'out of sorts' and 'pouting' because Aiden announced his engagement," David said with a glower I couldn't read. "Like I'd be jealous over my brother hog-tying himself to some lady. Anyway," he added when Owen looked ready to interrupt again, "since the surface-level adoption record search, both open and closed, seemed to be a no-go, I decided to run another, deeper search on the deep web, you know, in case there was anything sealed, or, you know, not on the up-and-up."

"Deep web?" I asked.

"You know, the part of the internet that's not really indexed by search engines. Usually it's pretty boring stuff, but it's where password-protected pages and encrypted networks and databases hang out. It's not really sketchy, not like the dark web, but—"

Owen cut him off. "Maybe we should save the internet-security lecture for another time?"

"Right," I said, but I made a mental note to learn more about hacking and network security stuff. It was kind of fascinating.

"Anyway," David said, brushing his bangs away from his face, "I set the search parameters and had just found some records originating in Iran, Turkmenistan, Afghanistan, and Pakistan, when bam, the trap fucking blew up, and next thing I know, it's a race to wipe away any traces pointing to me or the council before the people on the other side of the trap could get too much information."

My mouth was completely dry, so it took a second to be able to say, "Did you make it? I mean, were you able to get away undetected?"

David curled his lip, and the skin around his eyes tightened. "Not entirely."

"Oh shit." Owen reached out, covering my hand with his.

"'Oh shit' is right. I had to ask Aiden, my perfect, brilliant programmer brother, to jump in. He was able to secure the council's data—"

"Thank goodness," Owen said.

"—but my system was completely mined. And now I have to go in front of the council to explain why I put everyone, the council, shifters in general, my family, at risk."

I drew my knees up, wrapping my arms round my legs. I couldn't believe the whole thing had taken such a turn.

"And the 'international terrorists' comment?"

David rolled his eyes like he thought Owen was being deliberately obtuse. "My system was compromised when I tried to hack into records for Iran, Afghanistan, Turkmenistan, and Pakistan. My brother is expecting

Homeland Security or the US Bureau of Counterterrorism to be in touch any minute now."

"Aiden's an alarmist," Owen said. "You're researching adoption records, not poking into anything terrorists would have a hand in. Your brother's just speculating due to the Iran/Afghanistan connection."

I squirmed a bit. "It's not completely unfounded. There are definite connections between illegal adoption schemes and human trafficking, and between human trafficking and terrorist groups."

"You don't think your situation has anything to do with any of that, do you?" Owen asked.

"No, of course not." Because, seriously, my situation was weird enough without terrorists. "The site you found, the one with the honeypot thingy, do you have anything to indicate it's connected to me?"

"Not really. It fit some of the parameters once I expanded to international adoption records, specifically in Iran. I warned you it would be trickier given where you were born, but I hadn't expected this. We don't have enough data, including proof of adoption or any of your birth information, to know if there's a likely connection or not. Will you be able to get me anything on that, by the way? Your birth certificate or medical information? If you can find the hospital you were born in, for example, it would narrow it down."

"You're still going to keep searching? Even after all this?" I waved my hand to encompass the room behind me. Hopefully he'd interpret that to include honeypots and data breaches.

His eyes narrowed, and I saw the steely determination that would likely serve him well as an investigative journalist. "I don't quit until I get the answers. No matter what."

Chapter Fourteen

IF I'd thought the car ride from the airport with my parents was painful, dinner with them was almost unbearable.

Owen tried. I gave him so much credit for his attempts at dinner-appropriate small talk. He asked my dad about his work. He even managed to sound interested in my dad's job as a continuous improvement consultant. Not that manufacturing technology was particularly exciting. Neither of my parents seemed to know what to think of this charming friend of mine. Several times I saw my dad glance between Owen and me, his expression full of questions I couldn't decipher.

Things got really tense when Owen asked about Iran. "Yusuf says he was born in Tehran. Is that where you two met?"

They exchanged looks. I don't think I'd ever noticed before how often they had these silent conversations. Was it a new thing, or had they always done it and I'd just been oblivious?

"Yes," Mom said. "We met while Joseph was working there. I was a student." She paused, then said, "You call my son Yusuf. Are you, as they say, sucking up?"

"Mom!" I dropped my fork.

Owen grinned. "Nah. When he first introduced himself, he said his name was Yusuf. It kind of stuck. Besides, it's a great name. And since nobody else calls him it, it's kind of a nickname, just between the two of us." Color spread across his cheeks.

If anything, my mom looked even more concerned.

Owen ate a bite of broccoli.

I racked my brain for something to talk about.

Dad raked his serving of rice from one side of his plate to the other, like it was one of those Zen sand garden things.

"Owen's dad is a doctor," I said when the tension got too thick for me to handle. I didn't just say the words, though. No, I blurted them out at about twice my normal speed and volume.

Three sets of eyes jerked to me.

"Oh, um, I mean, I wanted you to know I'd had a meeting with a local doctor." Remembering something Dr. Weyer said, I added, "You know. It's important to have someone local who is familiar with my medical history."

Dad paused his rice raking. "I'm sure he's a competent physician." I imagined he finished the sentence with "but he's not Dr. Mirza" at the end.

"Speaking of," Mom said before I could decide what, if anything, I should have said to my father's disparaging tone, "we made an appointment for you to see Dr. Mirza tomorrow."

For the second time over the course of the meal, I dropped my fork. "Why would you do that? I'm feeling—" I hastily substituted "all right" for "great." I still didn't need them to be aware of just how well I felt.

"It's been almost three months since your last appointment. Even if you are feeling better—especially if you are feeling better—regular checkups are vital." Dad laid his fork down.

"Besides," Mom added, "After all this time, Dr. Mirza is practically family. He misses you nearly as much as we do."

I could almost believe that. I'd been seeing him almost weekly for the last fifteen years.

"He mentioned there were some promising new studies in gene therapies—" Dad grunted, the words cutting off. I'm pretty sure my mom had kicked his shin.

"No treatments. No gene therapies. No appointments with Dr. Mirza. Not now. Not again."

"Joey," Dad began, but a look from my mom had him reining it in.

Mom reached across the table and patted my hand. "It's good to have you home. We've missed you."

Luckily we finished dinner a few minutes later. Owen started to help clear dishes before Mom shooed him away. "Guests don't help. Go. Relax. Joey will help."

Dad led Owen to the living room, saying something about baseball. To the best of my knowledge, my dad wasn't a particular fan of baseball. He could go on for as long as anyone could listen about hockey, but baseball was not his sport.

I stacked plates and carried them to the kitchen, knowing full well Mom really wanted to get me alone while Dad distracted Owen. I started the faucet running, then rummaged through the cabinet under the sink for dish soap.

Mom added the serving dishes to the sink and clucked her tongue. She nudged me aside with her hip. "We have a dishwasher."

We rinsed dishes and filled the dishwasher in silence. Mom grabbed a sponge and started wiping the already spotless countertop.

"What's going on, Mom?" I took the sponge from her.

I was so much taller than her, I could have rested my chin on the top of her head. It made me grin to think of it. And because it made me happy, and because I was learning the importance of touch, I wrapped my arms around her, hugged her close, and rested my chin on the top of her head. Because I could.

"I love you. You know that, right?" she asked, her voice muffled a bit by my chest.

I stepped back. "Yeah, I know, Mom. I love you too."

"You know you can tell us things. Things you feel. Things about yourself."

Things I felt? Did she think I was keeping secrets? Well, to be honest, I guess I was. Lots of secrets. But I couldn't explain to her about the Asiatic lion inside me. And if I couldn't mention shifters, I couldn't explain about the healthy thing. And there was no way that was what she meant. "Sure, Mom."

"You know we, your father and I, love you no matter what."

"Uh-huh." I stepped back so I could see her face. I had her eyes. Not the color, so much, but the shape. And her nose. "What are you getting at?"

"I like Owen." She said it with a decisive nod, as though daring me to argue.

"Um, okay. Good. I mean, he's a good guy. A good friend."

"I am not ignorant, you know. I have traditional beliefs sometimes, but I'm not narrow-minded. I voted for Hillary."

What the hell?

She looked at me, waiting for a response.

"Okay." I honestly had no idea what else to say.

"It is okay if Owen is your boyfriend."

I choked.

"I only wish you had felt comfortable enough to tell your father and me that you are gay."

I sputtered.

"That's not... I mean...." I stopped to clear my throat. "He's not my boyfriend."

She crossed her arms over her chest. "You cannot lie to your mother, Joey. It is okay to be gay. Your father's mother's sister had been in a lesbian relationship for forty years."

I scrubbed my hand over my eyes. "Okay, I mean, yeah, I'm gay, or maybe bi, I don't know for sure, but Owen's not my boyfriend."

"Why not? If you do not care for him in such a way, you had better watch your actions. It would be cruel to string him along. He clearly has feelings for you."

"I don't... that's not...." I needed to stop sputtering. I had no doubt Owen had feelings for me—*friendly* feelings. Mom couldn't think it was more than that. "Do you really think?"

Oh man. The hope in my voice was painful to hear. I couldn't make myself retract the question.

"Joey. I often have regretted that you did not have the same experiences growing up as other kids your age."

"I'm twenty-one, Mom, hardly a kid." It absolutely wasn't the point, but the regret in her tone was even more painful to listen to than the hope in mine.

"Shh." She patted my cheek again. I should have found it annoying, but it was more touch than I was used to from her, and I found I reveled in it now. At least enough not to object to being treated like a child. "You will always be a kid to me. Twenty-one is nothing. Someday you will be as old as me."

I hugged her again. "You're not old."

"And you cannot distract me. I want you to know there is nothing I regret more than you not having the childhood you deserved. But it's nice to see you in the blush of first love."

"Love?" I croaked and pulled away to gape at her.

Her eyes crinkled, and I couldn't help but grin back at her. "Fine," she said. "A crush, at least."

"This is embarrassing. Is this what it's like for normal teenagers? I'm glad I missed this. I don't think I could have handled the angst as a thirteen-year-old."

We leaned against the counter together, her shoulder pressing in my elbow.

"You seem happier," she said after a moment. "It makes me happy to see it."

"I am happier."

The little wrinkle along her eyes, which moments ago had been crinkling with her smile, now tightened with regret. "We worry about you, your father and I, so far away."

"It's been good for me," I told her.

"I can see it is so, but I still worry. We want you to be happy, but we want you to be safe. It's hard to tell if you can be both."

"I get it, I do." I shoved my hands into my pockets. "But it's time I made the decisions affecting my life."

"I shouldn't ask, but can you see Dr. Mirza tomorrow? He's got the time, you're here. He's been so worried about you when you left. I have never seen him as upset as he was when we told him you'd gone to college so far away, refusing more treatment."

"Mom—"

"One more time, Joey. For our peace of mind."

I closed my eyes. "You don't play fair."

"Mother's prerogative."

I thought about how much I did not want to see Dr. Mirza. I thought about how much I detested the smell of antiseptic and rubbing alcohol. I thought about the invasive tests and unending discomfort. And then I thought about the sacrifices Mom and Dad had made to ensure I got the best treatment available. I sighed. "Fine. One more time. Then I'm done. Unless or until something drastic happens"—like turning into an Asiatic lion—"it'll be the last time."

"Thank you." She reached up to pat my cheek again. Nope, still not annoying. I captured her hand and held it to my heart.

IT was 3:00 a.m., and my stomach growled long and loud enough to wake me up from a fitful sleep. A glance at the clock reminded me it had been less than two hours since the last time I'd looked at it. My stomach growled again, this time accompanied by an ache that was starting to feel familiar.

Mom's bland dinner, while meeting some very specific nutritional requirements, was not nearly enough to sustain me. Not at the rate I'd been eating lately. I flipped the blankets back and swung my legs over the side of the bed. I had no idea what was in the kitchen, and if whatever it was would require some kind of complicated preparation process. I hadn't gotten beyond microwave meals and ready-to-eat deli selections in my attempts to fend for myself in the kitchen.

I'd barely stepped on the slate-tiled floor when Owen's voice from the living room stopped me. "Still wandering around in the middle of the night, I see."

I spun to face him, heart thundering. "Damn, Owen. You scared the crap out of me."

The growl my stomach let out was probably loud enough for a nonshifter to hear from the other room. Owen snorted. "Figures. Midnight snack craving, not insomnia, has you wandering the halls this time."

"At least in part. Tonight's dinner wore off several hours ago." I'd never thought to ask Owen about his own metabolism. If I was hungry, he probably was too. "Oh man, Owen. You're probably starving."

"I could eat," he admitted. "It's not as new to me, though, so I probably don't feel it as strongly. You, on the other hand, probably should have eaten at least twice what you did."

I shook my head, knowing he could see me as clearly as I saw him. Maybe clearer. He was a part-time owl, after all. "It would have been suspicious. Also, there were no leftovers, so Mom made exactly enough servings."

Owen came into the kitchen, and I nearly swallowed my tongue. He was wearing a white undershirt and boxers. It was the hottest thing I'd ever seen, even if the boxers had yellow-faced emojis grinning from the blue fabric.

"You going to raid the fridge? You can't let yourself get too hungry. It's dangerous."

I rolled my eyes. "Yes, Mom." I headed toward the fridge. "You want something? I have no idea what our options are. I can't cook, so we may be eating raw chicken or uncooked potatoes."

Owen's teeth flashed. "I'm a predator, dude. I've eaten worse."

That stopped me. "Right. It hadn't occurred to me. Does that mean you eat rodents and stuff when you change?" Another thought hit me. "You don't, like, eat small animals in human form, do you?" I had an absurd image of me in my human body tackling a wildebeest or whatever Asiatic lions ate in the wilds of India. Did they have wildebeests in India, or was that an African animal? It didn't matter. I wouldn't be killing or eating a wildebeest, for fuck's sake, no matter my form.

He grimaced. "Ick. Some things are easier when done as the animal. I mean, I could probably do it if I had to, like to survive or something, but I was kidding about the chicken. If I'm not wearing feathers, I'm not eating raw meat."

I opened the fridge but looked at Owen instead. "I'd like to see that someday. You as an owl."

"Someday," he hedged.

My stomach dropped. "Is it private? Did I make some kind of shifter faux pas by asking?"

"It's not that. I mean, there's some level of trust, I guess, but it's not really private. Not among shifters."

"Then what?"

He tugged at his ear, averting his eyes for a moment. "It's just, right now, it's better if no one shifts around you. Not until you get better control. And not unless it's someone your animal absolutely would not look at like prey."

"You think I'd hurt you?"

"Not on purpose."

"But you have to know I wouldn't. I'd never. Besides, you can fly. Even in my lion form, I wouldn't be a threat to you in the air."

"It's not just that. At this point it's completely possible, likely even, that anyone shifting around you would trigger your shift. And with the exception of the Bradys, no one could effectively stop you from hurting anyone else who might be around."

"So you do think I'm dangerous." I was beginning to think life was less complicated and hurt less when I didn't talk so much. I didn't know how to protect myself from all these conversations today, all the words spoken. Opening up made me vulnerable.

Luckily for me, I could ostrich with the best of them. "Let's see what we've got here." I turned my attention to the fridge.

Heat seared up my spine when Owen rested his hand between my shoulder blades. "It's just for a while, until things aren't quite as new."

I refused to look at him. I scanned the shelves. The pickings were pretty slim. "Aha! Hummus. And some carrots. No cooking required."

"That'll be good." His words were soft, and I regretted the loss of warmth when he dropped his hand.

I set the hummus aside and reached for the bag of baby carrots. "Oh, cheese. Extra protein, right?" I grabbed a few tubes of individually wrapped string cheese.

We carried the snack to the table. Owen sat next to me, which seemed a little weird with no one else there.

After three carrots loaded with scoops of hummus and two string cheeses, I felt a little less irritated. It was easier to call it irritation than hurt.

Owen dipped a carrot into the hummus. He examined the label. "Is hummus part of Iranian cuisine?"

"Nah. At least that's what Mom says. It's more common in Egypt, Israel, or Jordan, Closer to the Mediterranean." I cringed. "Sorry for the random trivia. Dad actually introduced it to Mom when I was little, not the other way around. We ended up researching it."

"I like trivia." Owen took a bite of his hummus-covered carrot. "You know what we should do now?"

I was unwrapping another string cheese. "What's that?"

"Find your birth certificate."

I fumbled the cheese. "Huh?"

"Now's the perfect time. We're up. Your parents are asleep. That was one of the things you wanted to do while we were here, right?"

"True." I paused, trying to figure out why I was so reluctant to do what I'd planned on doing. Guilt, I decided. It came down to guilt. So many questionable decisions lately had been made as a result of this mix of gratitude, obligation, and guilt.

I glanced at the big wall clock hanging over the couch. Nearly four. "We'll have to be quick about it. Mom is a bit of an early riser."

WE started in my dad's office. My dad was nothing if not organized. The room, which was meant to be a third bedroom, was wall-to-wall filing cabinets and bookshelves, with productivity, sustainability, and efficiency manuals lined up alphabetically by subject, and then further organized by year.

Owen pointed to a silver frame with a picture of me from when I was maybe four years old. It was summer and I'd been at a park. Mom got a shot of me standing at the top of the slide, posing like a superhero.

"This is the cutest thing I've ever seen." Owen scanned the shelves, probably looking for more pictures of me as a kid.

There weren't any. Nothing framed and put on display, at any rate. I'd started getting sick shortly after the park picture had been taken, and I'd refused to let my parents take any unnecessary photos after that. There were some family pictures over the years, but nothing like this happy, candid shot.

There was a great picture from my parents' wedding. They'd been married in Tehran about a year and a half before they moved back to the States with six-month-old me. I always joked that it was funny they had a honeymoon baby when they hadn't gone on a honeymoon.

I'd always loved this picture. It showed a much younger version of my dad sitting next to an equally young version of my mom. Even though my dad was an American citizen, they'd done a fairly traditional Persian ceremony. The bridesmaids held the traditional sofreyé aghd, a symbolic cloth used in weddings, over their heads while Dad stared at Mom in wonder. It was that look, the obvious awe on his face, that showed me my parents' marriage was based on love.

Owen sidled up to me and examined the photo. He pointed to a cluster of men in dark suits in the background of the image. "Dude, the men in your family are hot. Is this a cousin? This guy could be your twin."

"Not a cousin," I said, even as my brain latched on to idea that he thought someone who looked like me was hot. Which, if looked at logically, meant that he thought I was hot in turn. "Both Mom and Dad are only children."

Owen tapped the frame. "Well, this guy's a relative. You can't deny the resemblance. Maybe a second cousin."

"You know," I said quietly, sitting behind my father's desk so I could start going through his drawers, "I'm more confused than ever. I mean, David says there's no record of an adoption. Which would mean one of my parents would have to be a shifter. But clearly neither of my parents is a shifter, which means I'm not biologically related, so I have to be adopted. But a family picture of some random relative—and, yeah, now that you point it out, if I grew a beard, I'd look just like that guy—would suggest he is related after all. But both scenarios can't be true. I can't be a shifter but not be adopted. It's frustrating."

I pulled a drawer open with maybe more force than I should have. The contents inside shifted, banging against the sidewalls.

Owen and I stilled, holding our breaths. When there were no signs of stirring from my parents' bedroom, we relaxed. Dad's desk was one of those old-fashioned wooden ones, broad and probably six feet wide. The kneehole was a deep cavern that was blocked from view by a heavy front panel. It had taken three movers to put it into place when we'd downsized from the bigger house to the condo a few years ago. I shouldn't have been worried about the noise; it was too solid a piece of furniture to echo.

"I feel like there's a Sherlock Holmes quote that might fit the occasion. If we keep eliminating the possible, whatever's left—"

"No matter how improbable, must be the truth," I finished. "Except it's eliminating the impossible, not the possible."

"Yeah, but we're also talking about shape-shifters, so our understanding of impossible is already a little skewed."

"Point to you. Why don't you start with the cabinets by the door?" I indicated the first filing cabinet with a nod of my head. "Dad's anal about his files, so everything should be neatly and meticulously labeled."

I'd be the first to admit, searching through several drawers of my dad's information—including electric bills from twenty years ago—was not very exciting. I'd actually thought it would be fairly easy to find my medical files. I mean, they were extensive, and, unlike the decades-old utility bills, still sort of relevant.

I started on the other side of the room. In the bottom drawer of a three-drawer cabinet, I found something unexpected. Nothing as pertinent as adoption records or birth certificates or proof of the shifter gene—though that probably wouldn't be found in a manila folder. I found a container, shaped like a shoebox covered in floral paper, full of pictures. They looked like family photos from the last forty years. Some were formal, like school pictures, and some were candid shots of everyday life in Iran. Mom's memories, obviously. Though it wasn't the time, I flipped through some of them. Mom was very closemouthed about her family. She hadn't shared much of her—our—culture either. I asked her about it once. She said some things were better to remain buried in the past, and some memories and traditions were too painful when one had to sever those ties. I hadn't asked for more information because interpersonal communication wasn't my strong suit, and prying when someone had very clearly shut the door on the conversation wasn't in me.

Obviously a flaw I needed to work on.

I found a family-style photo with a man, a woman, and two kids. It was stilted in the way posed portraits always were. There was a boy, probably fifteen or sixteen, and a girl, clearly my mom, at maybe ten. I recognized the boy from the wedding photo, and without the beard, his resemblance to my mom—to me—was more obvious. She'd told me she didn't have any family, but this had to be my mother's brother.

"What'd you find?"

I hadn't heard Owen approach, too caught up in the treasure trove of family history I'd discovered. "Just some old photos." I returned the pictures to the box and tucked the whole thing back into the drawer. More questions. More secrets. But not what we were there for.

"You okay?" Owen clamped a hand on my shoulder. Like always, the touch helped me relax.

I leaned into the contact for a second. "Yeah. It's just… a lot." I licked my lips. "You finding anything?"

Owen's lips quirked. "Yeah. Lots and lots of information about medical supply manufacturing and the related efficiency and budgetary reports."

"Yeah, that's my dad. Super exciting, I know."

His hand slid down my back as he dropped his touch. It was a light graze, and probably not deliberate, but it caused things in my stomach to tighten. My breath hitched. "Um, we should probably, you know, keep looking." I wished my voice hadn't been quite so wispy, but my lungs had seized as goose bumps erupted along every inch of my suddenly overheated skin.

He moved away, and I probably imagined the quick flash of heat in his gaze as he did so.

I moved on to the next cabinet. I could tell I was getting closer to our goal because instead of the work-related files Owen had been riffling through, or the antique utility bills I'd found in the other cabinet, this one was full of important family documents. My gut clenched at the folder containing copies of my parents' wills. I quickly moved on; I couldn't even contemplate the idea of one or the both of them dying, not even in theory.

I moved to the second drawer in the cabinet. "Found it," I said softly, knowing Owen would be able to hear me.

He rushed over.

File after bulging file of medical records for one Yusuf Robert Franke, color-coded by year, broken down by specialist. Owen hissed in a breath. "Damn. I know you'd said you'd been through a lot, but seeing it all laid out like this…."

I smiled grimly, shutting the drawer. I opened the bottom of the three-drawer cabinet and showed him another whole stack of folders.

"I really want to hug you right now," he said.

The files went back twenty-one years. I backtracked until I found the one dated the year I was born. Yes, my dad really was that meticulous. The first few years of my life had skinny folders, with the typical kid stuff. Regular checkups. Stitches when I was three and cut my hand on a steak knife I'd somehow pulled out of the dishwasher when my mom's back was turned. Nothing major. I pulled out the oldest file, which contained my first visit to a pediatrician after we'd moved back to the US. I squinted at it. "Weird."

"What's weird?" Owen asked, still distracted by the number of medical files.

"There's nothing here from when we lived in Iran. Maybe they weren't able to bring all their records with? Or maybe they lost them?"

"Yusuf, your dad has records going back to 1980— when he was in middle school. I'm not sure he's lost anything in his life. And two of the cabinets I went through—all six drawers—have files from his time at MediCorp, which, based on what I saw, was the company he worked with in Iran. I think he even had dinner receipts."

And if Dad brought random receipts back to the States, he'd have brought any medical information on me. Owen didn't say it out loud, but I made the connection anyway.

"We might be looking in the wrong place," Owen said. "I mean, this is all your medical history, right? Well, when you were born, that would have been your mother's medical history, right? We might be able to find something there."

I tried to let his words reassure me. After seeing those pictures, there was no way my mother wasn't biologically my mother. I was the spitting image of her brother.

We both went statue-still at a subtle shift in the air. At first I didn't know what had happened.

Owen leaned close. He had to stand on his toes to whisper in my ear, "Someone's up."

My gaze darted to the open door of the office. Shit. Why hadn't we closed it? Because, my brain supplied just as quickly, it was never closed. That would have been suspicious.

I heard the lightest of footsteps coming from the hall.

Damn it. I couldn't afford to be caught. I had no excuse for both of us being in Dad's office. I slid the open drawer nearly closed, stopping before it could latch shut to avoid the clicking sound. There was a closet, but it was on the other side of the room.

"Behind the desk," I hissed, ducking and pulling him after me. The desk was broad enough to hide us, the front completely covered.

Owen tripped on my outstretched leg on his way down, crashing into me, knocking us both flat to the ground. He wasn't as tall as me, but he was solid muscle. The weight of him drove the air out of my lungs, leaving me gasping. He braced his arms on either side of my shoulders and sat up, giving me room so I could breathe. I gasped for an altogether different reason. He'd landed in such a way that his hips were cradled between my thighs, and the new angle pressed his abdomen solidly against my groin.

I gulped.

Owen watched me wide-eyed, lips parted.

Now really wasn't the time for this. But, oh boy, did my body jump up and tell me this was *exactly* what we should be doing, at *exactly* this moment.

Footsteps in the hall came closer. Mom—I could tell it was her by the softness of the tread—seemed to be heading for the kitchen.

"Your legs!" Owen mouthed the words and nudged my knee.

Crap. My feet were sticking out beyond the edge of the desk. I pulled my feet back, raising my knees, which in turn shifted Owen more intimately against me.

He gulped this time.

The scent of Mom's moisturizer wafted through the open door as she passed.

We held our breaths, not looking away from each other.

That kind of prolonged eye contact should have been uncomfortable. Too intimate. I'd heard the phrase *drowning in somebody's eyes* before. I'd laughed it off as overly romantic drivel. But, damn, I was seriously drowning in Owen's big amber eyes.

A kitchen cupboard opened and closed. Water ran.

My dick was as hard as it'd ever been. And from the flush on Owen's face, he knew it. I couldn't find it in me to be embarrassed.

A glass clinked in the sink.

Owen rocked into me, gritted his teeth, shifted back as though the original movement hadn't been intentional.

Mom took a couple more steps, then stopped somewhat abruptly. In my head I traced her route to the kitchen for a drink of water, then the return trip. Both routes would have her passing the living room and the couch where Owen was supposed to be sleeping. Had she noticed the empty sheets? Did she know Owen wasn't where he was supposed to be?

A few seconds later she continued to the hallway, her steps pausing again. But not here, not at Dad's office. She stopped a few feet farther down. My room. I squeezed my eyes shut, anticipating a knock or the *swoosh* of the door as she peeked into my room. But neither happened. Instead, she walked the last several feet to her own bedroom.

So my mother, who now knew I was gay, and who suspected I was in a relationship with Owen even though I denied it, now believed Owen and I were sharing a bed.

One the one hand, I had to give her credit for being so cool about it. On the other hand, my mom and I hadn't ever really talked about sex, let alone gay sex, or what the protocol was for overnight guests.

Breakfast was going to be awkward as hell.

Chapter Fifteen

OWEN and I stayed exactly as we were for almost five minutes. And I knew this because I counted each and every second while we waited a reasonable amount of time to make sure Mom had fallen back to sleep.

It was five minutes of the most exquisite hell I could imagine.

That effect Owen's touch had on me on a normal day? Yeah, it was exponentially worse—or better, depending on one's perspective—when it was a full-body connection, complete with intimate eye contact.

All my skin tingled and burned, like when I had a fever, but in a way that made me want to rub against Owen to increase the pressure. My heart beat at a faster rate. My breathing became erratic. And I yearned. I yearned for something I didn't think I could verbalize.

For something I'd never acknowledged in a real way before Owen.

"We should get up," I said when I finally remembered how my vocal chords worked.

"Are we going to keep searching?"

And, man, that campfire-smoke-at-midnight voice of his was the sexiest thing I'd ever heard when it was husky and soft.

I shook my head. "Maybe tomorrow night. It's too close to dawn, and I can't assume my mom is completely sound asleep."

Owen rolled off me, and I mourned the loss of his weight. He stood and offered me a hand up. I took it because, dark as the room was, I could see the way his emoji boxers tented, and it made my knees tremble. It was both sexy as fuck and intimidating as hell. That boner was for me. Me. I'd done that.

Owen hesitated at the door. "Well, I guess we should go back to sleep."

I nodded, though neither of us took a step.

With a lingering look at my mouth, Owen said, "Good night."

He took a single step past the threshold, and I grabbed his arm before he could turn to the living room and I could turn to my bedroom.

"Stay with me?"

The muscles of his forearm tightened.

"My bed is big enough for the both of us, and it'll be way more comfortable than the couch."

"Yusuf, I…. Your parents…."

"I'm pretty sure my mom already thinks you're in there with me."

He bit his lower lip, indecision visible on his face.

I took half a step back. I'd been pushing him, which hadn't been my intention. Just because some part of me was desperately urging me to keep him close, to explore the exhilarating tension between us, it didn't mean he was into it, or into me that way. Even the erection he was sporting could be as much to do with proximity to a warm body as with me specifically. "It's okay if you don't want—"

He stopped my words with a thumb across my lips. "It's not that. I want to."

"Then…."

"I need you to be clear about what you want, what you expect. I don't want to presume anything, or assume, or pressure you in any way."

I altered my grip so I could hold his hand instead of his arm. "Is it okay if I don't know what I want? I know I want *something*, but—" I stopped. This was going to get weird if we tried to have this conversation in whispers in the hallway of my parents' condo. "Look, can we go to my room and talk about this? Nothing more until we've made sure we're on the same page."

"Yeah, okay. That'd be good."

I kept hold of his hand and dragged him to my room, where we could shut the door and ensure at least a little bit of privacy from parental nighttime wanderings. We took up what I was beginning to think of as our regular positions on my bed. Me at the head, him at the foot, sitting cross-legged facing each other.

"Did you want to talk about what you found in there?" Owen tilted his head in the general direction of my dad's office.

"No. We'll deal with it tomorrow. We should talk about the other thing before I remember that talking and confessions are not something I'm good at and I freak out. If I don't do it now, I may not get the nerve to do it later."

Owen leaned forward, resting his elbows on his knees. "You don't have to tell me anything you don't want to."

"That's the problem, though. I want to tell you stuff, but then I get all caught up in my head and start to think maybe silent contemplation is the better approach. Less embarrassing."

"Well, if you're worried I'm going to judge you or laugh at you, don't. I want to know anything you want to tell me."

Well, he asked for it. "I'm twenty-one years old, and I don't know if I like guys, or if I just like you. I don't know if I'm gay or bisexual, or what. I've never been with anyone before. Never wanted to be with anyone. I've never been on a date. Never kissed anyone until you. And now that my body doesn't seem to be trying to tear itself apart from the inside out, I want things I'd never wanted before, and I don't know what to do about it. I dream about you, about being with you, and I wake up, shaking, and hot, and, holy shit, I'm going to shut up now." Because Owen was staring at me like I'd sucker punched him.

I crossed my arms protectively over my chest. "I'm sorry. I worried this would be—"

Owen lunged forward, capturing both my hands in his. It pulled my arms away from my chest but kept them crossed at the wrist. It was a little awkward, but I wasn't going to pull away to make it more comfortable. It would mean losing Owen's touch.

"There is nothing to worry about. I'm just trying to process everything."

"Any particular part?" I tugged experimentally at his hold. Not that I wanted to get away, but to see if he'd let me. He didn't. His fingers tightened, and something relaxed inside me.

"You've really never...."

I lifted my shoulders. "Honestly, I was so sick for so long, it wasn't like I met anyone. I barely saw anyone my own age, and even if I had, it's not like I'd have been able to date them. My parents kept me pretty sequestered at the advice of my doctor."

"And since you've been at Cody College, you've met more people your age. And none of them... attracted you?"

"Well, David is gorgeous in a too-good-to-be-true way, but I wasn't attracted to him. Mostly I wanted to claw his face off because you and he—" I shut up before I could finish that particular thought. Owen did *not* need to know about that.

Owen smirked.

"Jerk." I shoved him a little. Not enough to disconnect our hands but enough to jostle him a bit. "In all seriousness, the suspense is killing me. What are you thinking?"

He sighed. "Yusuf, I think you're hot. I've wanted you since the first time I saw you. And that's just your looks. After the first time we played chess, I wanted you even more. Because of who you are. The knowledge that you want me too, and that you've never been with anyone— and I don't mean just physically—is a huge turn-on. But I'm worried you're caught up in the newness of everything. I don't want to take advantage of that, of you."

This time I did push him away, breaking his grip. "Oh, screw you. I may be inexperienced, but it doesn't mean I'm stupid. I may not know a lot about sex and relationships or whatever, but it doesn't mean I don't recognize and understand my own reactions. You don't get to take that away from me. I don't need anyone telling me what to do or how to feel."

He took a deep breath, holding it for a moment. "You're right. You're absolutely right. But you need to know, if we start something and you decide it's not worth it, that I'm not who you want, it's going to kill me. Because you *are* who I want, and I don't think I could handle being with you, then having you walk away."

And if that didn't turn me upside down and inside out.

It took me a solid twenty seconds to process it completely and figure out what I needed to say. Finally I said, "I can't make any promises for the future, but I can tell you I like the way I feel around you. I like the way touching you, and you touching me, makes me feel. I want to feel more of it, to experience all these things I've never done before. I don't want to use you, and I don't think I am, but I don't want to push you into something you're not interested in."

"So what you're saying is I'm hesitating in order to protect you, you're hesitating in order to protect me, and in the end, we both want the same thing."

"Pretty much."

He reached out, relinking our hands. "What do you want tonight?"

"Maybe start with kissing—I like the kissing—and play the rest by ear?"

"I like that." He grinned wickedly, pulling me close. "I like that a lot."

The warm puff of his breath before our lips met was as much a turn-on as the weight of him pressing into me earlier. A sign of connection, of intent, igniting something hotter, something darker, deep in my chest. And my gut. And, let's face it, my groin. The careful way he fitted our mouths together brought my blood to a simmer. Then his control slipped, and his touch was less careful, more frantic, and the simmer turned into a full-on boil.

I groaned into his mouth, nipping at his bottom lip, demanding more, even though I couldn't exactly define what *more* would consist of. He came up to his knees, crowding closer to me, his hands digging into my lower back, dragging me closer. We were stopped by my position—sitting cross-legged kept my knees between us, and I wasn't flexible enough to pretzel myself into a position that would bring our bodies against each other. I needed closeness more than I needed to breathe. It was uncoordinated and random, and at one point I fell forward, causing our teeth to bash together, but eventually we maneuvered ourselves around so we lay on our sides, face-to-face.

Now that our posture was conducive to comfortably making out, it became a thing of frantic touches and desperate embraces. I didn't have time to worry that I didn't know what I was doing or that my life was mired in secrets. All I knew was *want* and *need* and *touch* and *feel*. Like shifting into a big cat three weeks ago, I was caught in the moment. In the visceral.

Owen's skin was soft and covered with muscle that was anything but. I pressed the tips of my fingers against the swell of his biceps. There was almost no give at all. I became obsessed with the dips and arcs of Owen's body, and I was determined to discover each and every layer. For his part, Owen seemed content to let me play, arching his neck to give me access to more skin. I followed the curves of his arm, up over the shoulder, skimming his throat, and down along his chest.

His shirt was in the way, so I tugged and yanked until he was free from the soft cotton. Now all the skin and strength of his chest were at my disposal. I flexed my fingers into the solid slabs of Owen's pectorals, digging in a bit with my nails. He arched, hissing in a breath, increasing the pressure. I did it again, a sharper scrape with my nails, and he groaned my name.

"I had no idea." I lifted my hands, enthralled with the pale half-moon arcs my fingernails had left in his skin. I ducked close and licked the marks I'd left.

"For someone new to all of this," Owen said, nearly panting for breath, "you seem to know what you're doing." He palmed the side of my face and urged it up until we were kissing again.

I loved this. The heat, the desperation, the connection. I had to touch everything, to see everything. A light dusting of blond hair trailed from his chest, down past his abs, until a thin line disappeared behind the waistband of his boxers. His nipples were tight little nubs I wanted to touch and tease and bite. I wanted to nibble kisses down his back. I wanted to wrap my hands around his dick and see if he felt different than I did down there.

"What can I do?" I asked, eyes raking over the exposed flesh and tented cotton boxers. I wanted to do this right, and if I was being honest, my brain was having trouble picking any one place to start.

Owen scraped his teeth along my jaw. "Seriously, Yusuf, if you ditch the shirt, I'm pretty sure you can do anything you want to me."

I wasted no time in ditching the shirt. Once it was gone, I pushed Owen onto his back, straddling his thighs. I hooked my feet over his shins and manacled his wrists with my hands so I could push them over his head. He lay sprawled and vulnerable below me, but he didn't seem to care about the submissive position. I knew he wasn't submissive in general and adored him for letting me restrain him with my body this way, even though I had no idea why my instinct was driving me toward it.

I buried my face at his throat, rubbing my nose and cheeks along the underside of his jaw and down his neck. The scratch of his beard stubble triggered a more primal reaction. I found the narrow ridge of his collarbone and bit. Owen's reaction was immediate; he arched into the bite, groaning. The motion had his lower body bowing up into mine. And holy shit, that meant he pressed into my erection, and I nearly came unglued.

Everything had been fine as long as I was focused on exploring him and seeing what kinds of reactions I could draw from him. But that one sensation was bigger, more powerful, than anything I'd yet experienced.

I lunged for his mouth, kissing and licking at his lips until they opened; then there was the slick glide of tongue on tongue. My body flared to life, want burning through me, stronger, more immediate than before. He met my passion, angling his jaw to deepen the contact, sucking on my tongue. It was sloppy and wet and completely addicting.

We broke away when oxygen became a necessity. While he gasped for breath, I clamped my mouth to his neck, sucking the delicate skin between my teeth, biting down until he hissed and bucked under me. He tasted of salt and sweat and pine trees at midnight, and it wasn't enough to enjoy the flavor. I needed to mark him, to show everyone he was mine. I moved to the other side of his neck and repeated the sucking/biting thing that he'd enjoyed so much and that I seemed to need so desperately. He palmed the back of my head, pushing me closer, urging me on.

He dragged his hands down my back, raking his fingernails the whole way. I rocked into him, rutting against him, all animal instinct now. He grabbed my ass, urging me on. I wanted more skin, more contact, I grabbed his boxers and tore them off his body, the seams splitting.

"I don't know whether to be scared or turned on," Owen said.

His words, and the realization that I had actually ripped his underwear, something that required more strength than I thought I had, restored a bit of my control. I levered myself up so I could get a read on Owen's emotions. His eyes were wide and glowing, pupils completely blown. Sexy as hell, but... "Don't want you to be scared. Is this okay?"

Owen's smile was blinding. "More than okay. Just seeing a side of you I hadn't expected. A really, really hot side." He grabbed my shoulders, pulling me back down to him. One of his legs wrapped around my waist, which pushed our cocks together. I hissed out a breath. The friction was amazing, but it wasn't enough.

I leaned back, putting some space between us. Owen made a rough sound at the separation, which made me want to kiss him. It was an awkward business, kissing him while at the same time pushing my pajama pants down. After a brief struggle where they got tangled around my ankles, I finally kicked the thin flannel free.

We groaned in unison as I settled against him. He was hot and hard, and I wanted to sit back and see him, but moving away at this point would have been impossible.

Synapses firing, body running entirely on adrenaline and hormones, I rutted against him, chasing something just out of reach.

It was the most amazing thing I'd ever felt.

It wasn't nearly enough.

"Help me. I want—" I didn't have the words to fully express what I wanted.

Owen knew. He reached down and took both our dicks in his hand, rubbing our shafts together.

"Fuck yes. This. This." I arched over him, thrusting into his grip, scraping my teeth over the taut skin of his shoulder. I covered his hand with mine so we were both pumping and caressing.

He rolled his hips in time to mine, and together we created a rhythm that was going to destroy me.

It was heat and friction and a pleasure so intense that when it overwhelmed me, my vision clouded, first flashing white, then fading to green. I growled, biting Owen, fangs piercing the skin and embedding in the muscle where neck met shoulder. Owen stiffened below me; then the wet heat of his release joined mine, coating our hands.

"Holy fucking shit," Owen gasped a while later.

By slow degrees my mind came back online. I'd fallen on top of Owen, covering him from head to toe thanks to the extra inches I had on him. I needed to move before he suffocated. I opened my mouth to say something, but the iron tang of blood on my tongue had terror and nausea roiling through me.

Horrified, I reared back and stared at the puncture wounds in Owen's skin. I pushed away, crashing to the floor. "Oh no!"

I wiped my wrist across my mouth, shame overwhelming me at the red stain.

"I'm sorry. I'm so sorry. I don't know why—" I jumped up, eyes frantically searching my room. "First aid kit. We'll clean it and bandage it. Unless—do you need stitches?"

Owen sat up, looking concerned but not angry. He probed the wound but didn't seem too upset. "Relax, Yusuf. It's fine."

"It's not fine! I *bit* you. You're *bleeding*. I think there's a first aid box in the bathroom. Just let me—"

He slid off the bed, crouching next to me a second later. I couldn't tear my eyes away from the pierced flesh. I'd done that. I'd hurt him. With my fucking teeth. Pressure built behind my eyes, and I had to blink away the sting before I broke down. Owen cupped my face in his hands, forcing me to meet his gaze instead of focusing on his injury. "I'm okay. We'll clean it up and everything will be fine."

I swallowed. "But—"

"It happens," he said. "We've got an animal inside us. And as human as we are, sometimes the animal comes out."

"I lost control." It was a hoarse whisper, full of regret and fear.

"Yeah, but to be fair, things were pretty intense." Owen stroked my hair away from my face, his expression gentle and understanding.

My heart started to slow to a more regular rhythm. "I don't want to hurt you."

"You won't—"

I covered his lips with my finger. "I don't want to hurt you, not like that, not when I'm not in control. When we get back to Cody, we'll need to track down Buddy. That way, when we do this again, if—when—I bite you again, it's going to be because you and I both like it, and there won't be broken skin."

He pressed his forehead against mine. "Good. That's... good. Because the biting? I want that. I think I've discovered a kink. But, yeah, maybe no blood."

Chapter Sixteen

"ARE you sure you want to do this?" Owen kept glancing at me as we walked to the nearest "L" station.

I wasn't sure if he was asking about the trip or the mode of transportation. So my answer, when I gave it, applied equally to both options. "Yes." There was enough doubt in my voice to also apply to both options equally.

After a horrifyingly embarrassing breakfast with my parents, during which my mom's gaze kept darting to the neatly folded bedding on the couch, my parents had wanted to drive me to Dr. Mirza's office. Not only did I not want to face the speculation in Mom's eyes, I needed to do this on my own. She'd guilted me into seeing Dr. Mirza one more time, for her peace of mind, but I wasn't going to make it any more like old times than I had to. Owen had offered to stay behind, either at my parents' condo or in a coffee shop while I kept my appointment. I'd vetoed that one immediately. With him there, I had a built-in excuse to get away from Dr. Mirza as soon as possible and to delay my return to my parents' place.

I'd sounded so confident when I told my parents and Owen that we'd use public transportation to get to Dr. Mirza's office. We could do this. Millions of people, including children, competently navigated Chicago's transportation system every day. I was a capable adult. I could do it too. Even if it did require an app on my phone with step-by-step directions.

My palms sweated, and I didn't think it had anything to do with the anxiety of using public transportation for the first time. And until Owen pried my arms away from my chest, I hadn't realized I'd fallen into my self-protective posture. He pulled me to a stop on the sidewalk.

"What's going on? Why are you so worried about this appointment? You said it's just a checkup, right?"

I didn't even know where to start. Past or present? Probably better to go with the immediate. "I'm healthy, now, right? I mean, I feel better, I look better. There's nothing to set me apart from any other twenty-one-year-old."

Eyes widening in understanding, Owen said, "Right. That could be awkward."

"And I can fake it a little with him, but what if he wants to take a blood test? I didn't ask your dad if it'll be obvious to a doctor now that I've actually shifted. I mean, will my hormone levels or whatever be different?" I started walking again, my steps as rushed as my words.

Owen had no trouble keeping up with me. "You're just going as a courtesy, right? Refuse any tests."

"It's not that easy," I muttered. "I mean, yes, it is, but you don't understand."

Owen dragged me to a stop again. "Yusuf, are you afraid of this doctor?"

"No. Yes. Sort of but not really." I averted my eyes and tried to wrangle my emotions so I could explain to him why I was acting like an anxious freak. "I've been seeing Dr. Mirza since I was five. That's when I started getting sick. After a bunch of tests came back indicating a likely autoimmune condition, my pediatrician referred me to a specialist for more in-depth care. At that point, Dr. Mirza became my primary doctor, coordinating all of my medical exams, tests, therapies. All of it. He's been a part of my life for fifteen years. My parents look at him as practically one of the family."

"But you don't?"

I tucked my shoulders in. "He's not a very warm person, if you know what I mean. Never mean. Never cruel, but kind of distant. He's my doctor, a researcher, not my uncle, so of course he's going to be a little distant. But sometimes it felt like the answers, the science, came first. Not me as a person. He didn't care if the treatments were painful or scary. I was a little kid, scared a lot, and he made my parents stay away long periods of time. When you're eight, you don't care about compromised immune systems, you want your mom to kiss your booboo and make it better."

Owen squeezed my hand, sympathy blazing in his eyes.

"I used to have nightmares about him and the tests when I was a kid. As an adult," I continued, "I understand. Intellectually, I understand he was doing his job, doing his best to help me. And I know it's not fair to hold it against Dr. Mirza that my life kind of sucked for so long. But sometimes it's hard to forget the scared little kid who was subjected to things no kid should have to face."

I looked at my phone, noticing the time. "We've got to keep moving. If we don't get to the 'L' stop on time, we'll miss the train."

"Just a second." Owen moved to stand in front of me. He planted his hands on my shoulders and looked up at me solemnly. "I'm sorry you had to go through that." Then he stood on tiptoes and looped his arms around my neck, giving me a back-crushing hug.

I buried my face in his flyaway hair. "I think that's why I struggle with some of the shifter things. I blame the lion inside me. If it weren't for the damned shifter gene, none of this would have happened."

Owen stroked along my spine, an up-and-down motion that was more soothing than anything had a right to be. "You'll need to accept your lion in order to control your shift. You could be dangerous otherwise." There was an apologetic note to his voice.

"I know." I sighed.

He held my hand the rest of the way to the train stop, all through the train ride, and during the three-block walk to Dr. Mirza's office.

Nora, the woman who'd manned the reception desk for as long as I could remember, greeted me. "Dr. Mirza is finishing up an appointment. He'll be right with you, Joey." She reminded me a bit of my mother. She was maybe a few years older, and not Persian, but she was short and softly rounded and had a gentle smile. Owen stiffened when he saw her.

I shot him a glance.

He shook his head, then mouthed the word "later" while we took seats in the small waiting room.

Dr. Mirza's waiting room was empty, though I'd never seen it any other way. It was sparsely furnished with half a dozen utilitarian padded chairs and a center coffee table with an assortment of magazines on it. I sat on the edge of my seat, knee bobbing, fingers freezing. There was something I wasn't used to here. A bitterness to the air, an underlying rot that slid over the normal scents of antiseptic cleaners and hand sanitizer. A layer of dust on the fake plant in the corner.

Then I remembered. I had shifter-augmented senses. I was just noticing things I hadn't before.

The jittery, skin-too-tight feeling that had me wandering the corridors of Matthison Hall at three in the morning was back and worse than ever. A sense of wrongness seeped through the room, settling over me like a greasy rain. I jumped to my feet.

Owen touched my forearm. "You okay?"

I jammed my fists into my jeans pockets and shrugged. "Antsy.'"

"Your face is really pale. Maybe we should leave—"

His phone chirped. Half a second later, mine dinged.

Our eyes met and we both reached for our cell phones.

"David?" Owen asked.

"David," I confirmed, after viewing the display. He'd sent the same note in a group message: *CALL ME ASAP.*

"Now what?"

"I'll call—" Owen started to say, but Nora stood, calling my name.

"Dr. Mirza will see you now."

I glanced from my phone to Nora and then to the door leading to the exam rooms. David's text flashed in its little green bubble.

"Joey?"

Owen stood. "I'll step out to call David. You go in for your appointment. We'll both be quick."

My stomach roiled, but I nodded.

He reached up, clasped his hands around my neck to pull me down, then planted a hard kiss on my lips. "You've got this. He can't hurt you anymore."

I ignored Nora's considering gaze as I followed the same path I'd taken almost once a week for more than fifteen years. When we reached an examination room, I stopped. "We can meet in his office. There won't be an exam this afternoon."

"But Dr. Mirza—"

"I'm only here as a courtesy," I said, remembering Owen's words. "We'll have a discussion but no tests."

"But—"

I ignored her and headed farther down the hall.

She scurried ahead of me, flinging herself in front of the office door. "Let me announce you first."

My phone signaled another incoming text. "Fine. I'll wait here." I leaned against the wall opposite Dr. Mirza's door, checking my phone while she slipped into the office. It wasn't David, as I'd assumed. It was Owen. *Danger. Don't go.*

A broad hand swiped my phone from my hand before I finished reading.

I jerked my head up, lunging for my device. "What the hell?" I stumbled back a step, when I realized I was facing a huge dude in a black suit. He looked like a cross between a Secret Service agent and an MMA fighter. He was as tall as I was but twice as wide, with muscles on top of his muscles. And he held a scary freaking handgun.

"Get in my office, Joey."

Little things came more sharply into focus. The bitterness-and-rot combo I'd smelled in the waiting room was coming off Dr. Mirza. There was a sharply cold edge of calculation in his gaze when he looked at me I'd never noticed. This was a man I'd spent time with, years with, and I'd only ever seen the outside-facing image he'd wanted me to see. This man, the bitter, calculating one, was the real deal.

My skin throbbed and itched. My vision started to go a little green around the edges, and my gums ached.

Shit. My lion wanted out in the worst way. He'd recognized something, sensed something, and was convinced we needed him to step in and protect us.

That was probably a very bad idea. Asiatic lions should not run loose in the city. And there was no doubt in my mind that if I let the lion out long enough to deal with Dr. Mirza, there was a very good chance he'd hit the streets. When it came to fight or flight, as evidence had recently proven, flight won. My instinct was always to run, to escape.

"Dr. Mirza? What's going on?" My voice was harsh with the effort required to act normal, as if there wasn't a three-hundred-pound cat waiting to pounce.

"You're looking well." Dr. Mirza stood and strolled around his desk. He stopped when he was a few feet in front of me. "You've gained weight."

"You've heard of the freshman fifteen, right?" My heart thrummed sickly behind my ribs.

"Somehow I don't think yours is the result of frat parties and pizza, is it, Joey?"

He knew. Somehow, Dr. Mirza knew what had happened.

"Fresh mountain air. It does wonders."

"You didn't used to be so mouthy."

"Dr. Mirza, can you tell me what's going on? I'm a little freaked-out by everything here. I'm not used to men with guns confiscating my cell phone."

"If you hadn't developed such a stubborn streak, none of this would be necessary."

When I didn't respond—though he couldn't have expected me to—Dr. Mirza said, "When did you discover what you were?"

"I don't know what you mean."

He tipped his head toward the Secret Service MMA fighter.

The Secret Service MMA fighter punched me in the gut.

I fell to my knees, hands clutched protectively over my stomach. The hit had knocked the wind out of me, and the pain blossomed throughout my torso. Nauseating and infuriating. My muscles spasmed and strength and fury unfurled inside me. I had to stay hunched over on the ground, not just because it was hard to breathe or because my stomach hurt where the goon with a gun had sucker punched me. No, I struggled to hold on to the shift.

"What the fuck, man?" I glared up at Dr. Mirza. I barely recognized my own voice, guttural and deep as it was.

"If you lie, there are consequences."

"I don't know what the hell you're talking about."

Dr. Mirza nodded at the Secret Service MMA fighter again. He pulled his hand back to deliver a downward swing toward my huddled body.

There was a sting of flesh against flesh as his fist, instead of landing across my face, smacked into my palm.

Holy crap. I'd seen stuff like that in movies but never thought I could do something so badass. I tightened my grip around his balled fist and squeezed. At first he didn't seem affected by it, but as bones and ligaments started rubbing against each other, his face paled.

I shot a glance at Dr. Mirza, who watched on with… satisfaction?

Slowly I stood, pushing back against the Secret Service MMA fighter's arm until he had to back up or risk me getting all up in his face. And I had the strength of a three-hundred-pound Asiatic lion inside me. He did *not* want me in his face.

The black-suited man sent his own glance toward Dr. Mirza, looking for directions.

While he was still stunned by my grab, and maybe worried about all those little bones in the human hand, I snatched the gun from his opposite hand. Why hadn't he used it on me?

"I had no idea you could be so fierce. You've ruined my research. I should be pissed. But to see what a difference it makes, from even a few months ago to now, is astounding."

"What research?" I ground out.

"Why, so we can create human-animal shape-shifters, of course. They would make the perfect soldiers or mercenaries."

My grip went slack, and the Secret Service MMA fighter pulled free. He glared at me, massaging his hand, but he stayed out of my reach.

"Excuse me?" They wanted to *create* shifters? My knees started to shake. "Is that… that's not… I didn't, I mean, I don't…."

"You really have changed these last months. I can't wait to run tests. How much stronger are you?"

I sputtered. "You mean you knew? All along, you knew what I was?"

"Of course."

"So you know why I was so sick."

"Yes."

Static buzzed and crackled in my ears, muffling all other sounds. Rage, like a burning tsunami, rushed through me, and I roared. It wasn't a human sound, not at all. It was a full-on animalistic sound, carrying with it all the fury and pain of fifteen years of near torture. I charged forward, hands extended and curled like claws. In fact, the fingernails had even started to thicken and grow into sharp points.

Secret Service MMA fighter guy, taking his role as bodyguard and hired muscle seriously, jumped to intercept. Muscles twitching and bulging, I caught him by the neck and held him one-handed, with his boots hanging two feet off the floor. I snarled, baring my teeth.

"His eyes," Nora gasped, cowering behind Dr. Mirza.

I didn't care about my eyes. I was acting on feral instinct and years of pent-up anger.

If I had to eliminate this threat before I could get to Dr. Mirza, so be it. I squeezed, feeling the man's skin shift over his esophagus and the curving edge of jawbone. He clawed at my hand, gurgling.

Dr. Mirza watched on dispassionately. "I'd prefer it if you didn't hurt Paul."

I sneered at him. Paul, if that was the Secret Service MMA fighter's name, was turning bright fuchsia.

"You don't want anything to happen to your boyfriend, do you?"

"Boyfriend?" I loosened my hold enough for Paul to suck in a quick breath. He still clung to my forearm in an attempt to take pressure off his neck. I wasn't quite ready to let him go completely, but I was willing to listen. I *needed* to listen. Somehow Dr. Mirza knew about Owen. "What about him?"

Dr. Mirza sent a chilling smile toward Nora. "It seems you were right about the importance of the boy."

"What about him?" I repeated. The words slurred, and I noticed my teeth had started to change, my canines hanging lower, growing sharper. My fingers tightened again on Paul's throat.

"If you hurt Paul, your new friend will be hurt."

"Leave him alone."

"Nora," Dr. Mirza said to his receptionist, "have the boy brought in."

Nora rushed past, staying as close to the opposite wall as she could manage.

"Owen doesn't have anything to do with this." Human. It was important to stay human. "I don't understand what you want." No matter what my instincts said, or how tight my skin felt, or what the green-hued vision indicated. Changing into an Asiatic lion while in the midst of a standoff with an evil doctor was a bad idea. I thought of Owen's hugs and of belly buttons. Those things that made me feel distinctly human.

I tried to keep my breathing steady. But then I caught something new on the air, a rich metallic scent that made my mouth water and my nerves sing. It was coming from Paul. Two of my claws had punctured the soft skin of his neck, and two trails of that tantalizing blood trickled to the collar of his black suit.

I rumbled, deep in my chest, eyes trapped on those two little wounds. It would be so easy. All I had to do was clench my fist and I could rip his throat out.

No. That wasn't me. Belly buttons. Owen's hugs. Italian subs.

The door to the waiting room burst open. Two men, wearing suits identical to the one the Secret Service MMA fighter wore, strode in, a struggling Owen held between them.

"Yusuf!" Owen pulled at the arms holding him, but the two goons kept their grips on his arms tight.

"Let him go," I growled, the lion in me surging closer to the surface.

"Release Paul," Dr. Mirza countered.

I snarled at him. "This is between us. Owen doesn't have anything to do with this."

"Doesn't he? We can always use another shifter for our research."

Owen stopped struggling. His face went white as he stared with new understanding at the tableau made by Dr. Mirza, the Secret Service MMA fighter, and me.

"You won't touch him."

"No?" Dr. Mirza sneered at me. "Owen means more to you than Paul does to me, which means I have the power."

Owen cried out as one of the goons holding him twisted his arm up along his spine. His knees bent, and he fell back.

The Secret Service MMA fighter gurgled, and I realized my grip had tightened around his throat again. I eased up, barely. "Let Owen go."

"They're not going to let me go, Yusuf." He sounded surprisingly calm—or maybe resigned—at the situation. "Now that I've seen them, and they mentioned research on shifters, I am as good as dead. Or, I guess in this case, a science experiment."

"He's smarter than you, Joey." Dr. Mirza reached into the open door of his office and pulled out a rifle. Before I had time to react, he fired.

Owen jerked.

I roared.

Owen slumped.

I shifted, the lion bursting out with a slash of claws and a flash of fang.

Nora screamed.

Dr. Mirza turned the rifle at me and fired again.

A pinch of pain in my haunch. Blurry vision. Muscles weakening.

My last thought before darkness descended was of Owen and of hugs and of belly buttons.

Chapter Seventeen

I CAME to in stages. First was smell. Antiseptic and rubbing alcohol. Then sound. Voices murmuring several feet away. Then feel. Smooth cold, like stainless steel, beneath me. Cool air from an air-conditioning vent blowing down on me. Then taste. A hint of copper on my tongue. Familiar and nauseating. Blood. Sight came last. Blinding white light, with subtly shifting shadows along the edge of my vision.

I tried to move, to look away from the light, but my head wouldn't budge. And neither would my arms or legs. This was different than the paralysis I'd experienced the night of my first shift. This wasn't my body trying to process something new and enormous. This was a stillness forced upon me from something outside.

I wiggled, trying to get a feel for what held me down. An inhuman huff escaped at the movement, and flashes of memory trickled through my brain, taking precedence over my worries about restraints.

The pop of the rifle.

Owen slumping to the ground.

Rage.

Shifting.

Blood.

Oh God. The blood.

Owen.

I yowled, my reactions more in tune with the primal side of me than the human. The lion in me didn't differentiate between the many gradations of pain, grief, regret, anger, frustration, guilt. It just knew hurt and the need to make it stop.

Owen had been shot, and I was stuck in shifted form, strapped down somewhere.

I cried out in anger. In mourning.

I struggled against the bonds holding me down. I was three hundred pounds of Asiatic lion. No way did they have anything that could hold me. I twisted, ignoring the straps digging into my chest, pulling at my mane. I flexed my paws, unsheathing my claws, trying to find something to tear, to slash. I jerked my legs, trying to pull them free from what held them. I barely noticed the sting of pain as the metal edge of one of the restraints dug in through the fur to cut into the skin, adding the odor of my own blood into the antiseptic-alcohol mix.

"Yusuf, relax. You need to calm down."

The midnight-smoke voice broke through the fog of rage and panic. Just a little at first, like a sunbeam peeking through storm clouds.

"*Yusuf.*" There was a hitch in the voice. I didn't like it when that person, that voice, was scared. And I didn't know if he was scared because of the situation or because of me. So I had to make sure he wasn't afraid of *me*. And then we could deal with the situation.

I had to concentrate. To calm down. To relax.

I stopped thrashing. I tried to force my breathing into a less frantic rhythm. I blinked a couple of times, which helped, even though it didn't make it any easier to see. It did give me a minute to understand that my inability to see was due to a high-wattage light shining into my face rather than some kind of rage-induced blindness. Eventually my heartbeat slowed and the fog cleared from my mind.

Throughout it all, Owen kept murmuring nonsensical words meant to quiet the beast in me.

Owen, who wasn't dead and was conscious and helping me, even though he wouldn't be caught up in this mess if it hadn't been for me.

I whined at him. I wanted to ask questions, like was he okay? What happened? Where was Dr. Mirza? But without human vocal chords, speaking was out of the question.

"You doing better?" he asked.

I chuffed, hoping he understood it as an affirmative. I whined again, trying to make the pitch go a little higher at the tail end of it. *Are you okay?*

"I'm all right."

I sniffed the air and could tell Dr. Mirza and his team had spent a lot of time in this room but weren't here at the moment. The voices I'd heard when I first woke up were distant, muffled by at least one layer of wall. Owen and I were alone now, but for how long? And even left to our own devices would only get us so far, given I didn't even know where we were or what the conditions were like.

I'd been through enough tests and procedures to say with some confidence I was in a surgery room or some other similarly decked-out chamber. The way Owen's voice had echoed told me the floor and walls were likely tile—nothing bounced sound around like tile and glass.

I did the questioning-whine thing again, hoping Owen would take the hint. I was strapped down and blinded by a bright light. Hopefully he was in a better position. He could talk, so he hadn't changed into his owl form. Not like when I changed—

Nope. Not going to think about that. Not yet. I didn't have time to deal with the blood on my hands—or claws, as was more correct.

Owen. I needed to focus on Owen. Who was awake and talking. And who could maybe see more than this damned bright light.

I growled. It was getting hard to maintain any semblance of control while annoyed in this form. Part of me wondered if submitting to the feral side wouldn't be easier. I writhed against the restraints, instinctively testing their strength, looking for weakness.

"I've got an idea," Owen said hesitantly. "A way you can get free from the straps there. But it doesn't get us much closer to getting away."

I grunted, jerking my head up and down, trying to tell him to get on with it. If I could get away from the straps, I could see. And speak. And maybe actually do something.

"The straps holding you down, even the ones at your paws, are meant to hold you in your lion form, right? Your human form is smaller than your lion form in all aspects. If you shift to human, you'll be able to just slide out of the straps."

Yes! It made so much sense I couldn't believe I hadn't thought about it before. If I shifted, I could at least get more information and have a chance to plan an escape attempt. The lion might be bigger and stronger—I had to push away the Technicolor reminders of exactly what the lion was capable of—but human would be better suited to protect Owen. If I had better control of my shift, maybe I'd be able to shift back to lion if the situation called for it, but control was not something I could count on yet.

I sucked in a breath as deep as the strap across my chest would allow, closed my eyes, and willed myself to change. Nothing happened. I tried again. *Change, damn it.*

"Yusuf, relax. Remember who you are. What you look like. Your long fingers. Your height. Your belly button."

Belly button. Belly buttons and Owen's hugs. Those things that make me feel human.

The wave of energy overtook me. I had to fight to the surface and struggle to come through the other side. Muscles seized, lungs burned, and I pushed through. Finally, when I feared it wasn't going to work, or that I was going to tear myself apart from the inside out, I broke through, gasping for air. I jerked up, naked and shaking, drenched in sweat, tangled in industrial-strength straps—like those used to tow cars—and wires.

I knocked away the broad surgical lamp blazing at me from a nearby stand. I blinked to clear my vision, and then I immediately sought Owen.

Owen's torso had been secured to a straight-backed chair using more of those tow-strap things, and his arms and legs were bound with rope. His hair was a bit more tousled than normal and his face was pale, but other than that he looked okay.

I slid out of the too-loose restraints and tried to run to him, but my muscles still shook, so it was more of a stumbling lurch. "Why didn't you shift too? Like, the opposite of what I did? Owls are smaller. You could have gotten loose." I found the rope wound around his wrists and felt for the knot.

Owen hissed, jolting away from me, skin turning a sickly sort of yellow. "In the struggle I ended up with a dislocated shoulder," he managed to say. "Can't shift with a dislocated shoulder. Wing would be all messed up."

I threw up my hands, falling on my ass next to the chair.

"It's fine."

"It's not fine." He'd been hurt because of me. Because he'd come with me to a stupid doctor's appointment I hadn't even wanted to go to.

I leaned forward and got back to releasing him. This time I was much more careful about how I jostled his arm, which slowed me down. His left shoulder hung a little lower than his right, and knowing why it did had me fighting a desire to vomit. His bones weren't where they were supposed to be. I shuddered. It had to hurt, but Owen sat there, stoic.

I freed his arms and bent lower to get at his ankles.

The door to the surgery opened. "That's far enough. Can't have you getting too far ahead of yourselves."

I snarled under my breath. I hadn't paid enough attention to what was going on around us. I'd missed the distant rumble of voices going quiet. My only thought had been to get to Owen and come up with some kind of escape plan.

I was definitely not hero material.

Dr. Mirza stood in the doorway, the two goons who'd grabbed Owen behind him.

I swung around to crouch in front of Owen. It was small protection, but it was all I had at the moment. "David's sending help." Owen's voice was so low I was the only one in the room who had a chance of hearing it. Score a point for shifter senses. It was something, at least. "Just need to stall."

How? Why? I kept my eyes trained on the bad guys. I couldn't ask for more information. Subvocal commentary from Owen was one thing. Seeing me demand answers was something Dr. Mirza definitely wouldn't miss.

"Where's Nora?" I asked. I needed a distraction, and that worked as well as any.

"Taking care of Paul. Someone had to arrange for the disposal of the body."

My stomach lurched.

The pop of the rifle.

Owen slumping to the ground.

Rage.

Shifting.

Blood.

"Focus," Owen muttered behind me.

I don't know how he knew what I needed, but his voice, his presence, made all the difference.

"I don't understand what you want. Why are you going to all this trouble?"

Dr. Mirza shook his head. "Money, of course. Why else? I suppose there are other considerations, such as prestige and glory, but really, there's a lot of money to be had if someone such as myself can find a way to militarize shifters and their strengths."

"It's never a good sign when the bad guys explain their plan. It means they don't expect you to get out of it alive." This time Owen spoke loud enough for everyone to hear.

"Oh, I don't want you dead." Dr. Mirza's chuckle was, not to sound melodramatic, evil. "I can't study you as effectively if you are dead."

"Why were you studying me? I didn't even know I was a shifter."

"Half shifters are rare. Most of your kind don't breed outside of their species. We needed to track the evolution, so to speak. You were one of the variables we needed to watch. We needed to map your genetic traits as a half shifter whose ability to transform is repressed, to those of a half shifter who shifts regularly, to those of a full shifter."

"But… how did you find me? How did you know what I was?"

"I knew your parents."

Everything inside me froze. "My parents?" They couldn't have been involved. It would be one thing to have been adopted and not know it. But for them to actively participate in this kind of repulsive testing, while at the same time acting like they loved me? I shook my head, denying the possibility, even as my heart was being torn in two.

"Oh, not the Frankes." Dr. Mirza waved his hand in dismissal. "No, they don't know anything about this, do they? But then, they aren't your real parents."

"Not my parents?"

"Focus," Owen urged from behind me.

"It had taken us years to find a suitable shifter-human couple. Years. And then you were born and somehow your parents—your biological parents, for clarity—

managed to send you out of the country with the Frankes. We thought you were lost to us, until you were five years old and started showing symptoms of a repressed shifter gene. I took one look at you and knew. I didn't even have to see the results of the first blood test to know for certain. You look just like your father."

I couldn't breathe. Something heavy and tight, like the straps that had secured me to the exam table I'd woken upon, squeezed my chest. Green edged along my vision, and my gums throbbed. I wanted to lash out, to hurt him as he was hurting me. Not just the years of futile testing or the painful procedures. I wanted to pay him back for the heartache I faced now. My parents weren't my parents. They'd lied to me. *But they've loved me*, another voice whispered.

"Focus."

The green receded at Owen's voice. A little.

"If you've know where I was for the last fifteen years, known *who* I was, why didn't you do anything earlier?"

"It was the best possible scenario. We could keep you separated from other shifters, to keep proximity from triggering the change. Your parents trusted me, so I could do any number of tests on you to track the impact. And best of all, they paid for it."

"You are such a bastard. You took advantage of them."

He shrugged. "I had an assignment to complete. Do we really need to have the 'ends justifies the means' conversation?"

I narrowed my eyes at him. "One of these days I'm going to take great pleasure in—" I didn't finish the statement. The two goons, who'd stayed silent throughout the whole exchange, each took a step closer. Both held handguns of some description. They didn't look like dart guns; they weren't going to take any chances.

I couldn't shift and tear his face off, no matter how much I wanted to.

No, I needed to stall.

"Now that I've shifted, doesn't that mess up your tests?"

Dr. Mirza's smile widened, and dread slithered down my back like winter slush. "Not at all. In fact, this is perfect. We can now have what is, essentially, a before and after. If we can isolate the difference in your DNA from before to now, it might be the key to finding a way to create new shifters. Imagine having a soldier with your strength and speed? Or the ability to fly undetected over enemy lines? No, Joey, this couldn't be more perfect."

Stall.

"Shifters aren't indestructible, you know. If you've done testing, I'm sure you've figured out we don't have any special healing ability or superpowers. Sure, most of us can see a little better, but mostly we just eat more and turn furry every once in a while." Owen teetered on the edge of mocking and serious. A hair in the wrong direction, and he'd become a target. Again.

"But that's the best part." Dr. Mirza's enthusiasm landed somewhere between head cheerleader at homecoming and a sci-fi geek at DragonCon. "Your metabolism! What if the fast metabolism can be harnessed and turned toward healing? The potential is already there. If it can be targeted to specific functions, militarized shifters would be immensely valuable."

"So what was your plan for me?" I wanted to distract Dr. Mirza and his goons from Owen. He was doing something behind me with his freed hands. From my position in front of him, I couldn't tell exactly what. They hadn't noticed his unbound hands yet, and we needed every advantage if we were going to get out of this.

My life as an invalid hadn't prepared me for facing off with some kind of Bond villain.

"You're just going to steal me away to some secret research facility to poke and prod me for the next several decades?"

Dr. Mirza's mouth twisted. "Basically."

"You're not going to get away with it." Which is what every victim of every action movie ever said. "There are people who know where we are and will be looking for us."

Owen grunted softly. I shot a quick glance over my shoulder. Owen was slumped in the chair. I didn't have time to discover more, because Dr. Mirza caught my look and was turning his attention on Owen. I took a step forward, drawing his gaze back to me. The goons kept their eyes—and their guns—trained on me.

"You mean your parents. I've got a plan for them. They'll never know you're gone."

I stopped worrying about whatever Owen was doing. "Excuse me?"

Satisfaction rolled off him in palpable waves. It even had a scent, something cloying like overripe fruit. "A car accident, maybe. Chicago traffic can be dangerous, you know."

An ache built in my jaw, and once again the world around me was colored by a green haze. I stalked forward, ignoring the increased tension coming from the goons.

"Yusuf, focus." Quiet as Owen's voice was, I could hear the strain in it. I was able to regain a small measure of control. Enough that the green partially receded.

Then Dr. Mirza had to go and ruin it by saying, "Of course, a home invasion might be better. Give a good excuse for someone to destroy any physical files or records linking me to the Frankes."

"No." The word came out in a bass rumble that sounded inhuman even to my own ears. It was a command, plain and simple. Nonnegotiable. One I was willing to ensure no matter the risks.

I took another step forward. My control hung by a very thin thread. There was something to be said for simplicity. The lion running on instinct was a simple creature. Simple was easy. The lion saw a threat, eliminated the threat. The human psyche complicated matters with guilt and regret, with morals and conscience. My fingertips tingled, the muscles along my back throbbed.

Owen grunted again, then sucked in a breath.

One of the goons jerked his head to try to see past me.

"I should have taken care of them long before now, but the money was useful to our cause."

I snarled.

"Uh, Dr. Mirza?" one of the goons said.

"He won't hurt me. Will you, Joey? If you take another step forward, I will have them shoot the boy." He jutted his chin to the area over my shoulder.

"What if he does what he did to Paul?" the other goon asked.

Their fear was sour-sharp in the small room. I loved it. The lion was in the driver's seat now, and it wanted them to be afraid of us, of me. Their fear soothed and tempted at the same time.

I bared my teeth and hissed.

Dr. Mirza's fear scent blended with the other two. I grinned with feral satisfaction.

"Joey," he warned, "If you take another step closer, I will have them shoot your friend. Is that what you want?"

A new odor filled the room. Snow and pine and midnight. Owen. Deeper and richer than normal. A subtle shift of energy swept past my feet, crawling along the floor.

I took another step closer.

Dr. Mirza stumbled back. "Shoo—"

I pounced, wrapping my fingers around his throat like I had Paul's.

A gun fired.

With a screech, a grayish feathered form swooped past my head.

Another shot rang out.

An icy line of fire cut across my biceps.

I ignored the pain, tightening my grip, squeezing past the loose flesh of his neck.

He was weak. He was prey.

The goons hollered as a huge great horned owl dove toward them, talons outstretched. They ducked, covering their heads. The owl continued to harry them as much as he could in the small space.

Dr. Mirza's eyes bulged in his rapidly reddening face.

I dug my nails in deeper.

The lab doors burst open in a wave of complex scents, and half a dozen men in black tactical gear and black caps swarmed the room.

I roared. I would attack anyone who threatened my parents, Owen, or me. If these guys were part of Dr. Mirza's psychotic group, I needed to show them I wasn't intimidated by their gear or their guns.

The owl whistled, the sound breaking my concentration enough for me to notice something besides the apparent threat. The room was awash in the smell of fur and feathers, of tropical rain, desert breezes, and pine forests. The owl—Owen—settled on the back of the chair where he'd been held.

The men in black uniforms had the two goons hauled up and in handcuffs within seconds.

The tallest among them stepped toward me and Dr. Mirza. I snarled. He was going to take the doctor away. I couldn't let the man who'd tormented me almost my entire life, the man who threatened my parents, who threatened Owen, live. The only way to stop the threat was to eliminate the source.

Dr. Mirza gurgled, his hands clawing at my arm. His knees buckled, but I held him firm by the neck. With the lion's enhanced vision, I could see the blood vessels popping in his eyes, the deepening purple suffusing his skin.

The owl—Owen, I had to remind myself—flapped his nearly five feet of wings, alighting from the chair. It was an awkward movement given the enclosed space, but he managed to land on my shoulder. Tucking his wings down, he hooted softly, scraping the side of his beak along my cheek. Even with his talons biting into my naked skin, his touch comforted me and allowed me to regain a measure of control.

Throwing Dr. Mirza away from me was the hardest thing I'd ever done. But I did it.

Head lowered, I pressed my clenched fists against my thighs as I watched two of the men rush to secure the man who'd made my life miserable. I inhaled, sucking air deep into my lungs, then held it for a moment before letting it out.

Every nerve and instinct I possessed told me to destroy Dr. Mirza before he could do any more harm. Tendons strained, muscles tightened.

Owen cooed at me. The sound landed somewhere between a hoot and growl, and it centered me.

Focus. I needed to focus.

I swallowed, licking my lips. When I'd gathered enough control that I didn't think I'd snap at our rescuers, I said, "I need to call my parents. They're in danger."

The tall man at the front of the remaining team members pulled off the black cap. He'd been giving orders to others, something about securing the rest of the building, but at my words he focused the palest blue eyes I'd ever seen on me. "I'll send someone to pick them up."

Whether it was the adrenaline crash or a residual effect of the tranquilizer Dr. Mirza had used, my knees buckled. I landed hard on the floor. Owen hopped down next to me. "Hey, you." It was the first good look I'd gotten at the owl that was my friend. He stood about two feet tall, with his wings tucked in. He feathers were a mottled mix of gray and brown and white. The eyes, those amazing amber eyes, were 100 percent Owen. I trailed my fingers over the tufts of feathers that made up the great horned owl's "horns." "You kind of look like Thor," I said before I could think better of it. "You know, when he's wearing his helmet."

Owen cocked his head at me, grumbled a bit, then shifted into his human form.

He settled in at my side, both of us sitting on the cold tile floor. I pulled him close so I could bury my face in his neck, letting the familiar scent of him calm my nerves. "I was so scared."

He hissed, and I jerked back. "Shit. Your shoulder! How'd you shift? You said you couldn't—" I let my gaze examine every centimeter of flesh from collarbone to elbow. Except for a little swelling, he seemed mostly intact.

"I don't recommend trying to relocate a dislocated shoulder without medical supervision and probably drugs."

"You can do that?" I reached out to touch him but was too afraid of hurting him to follow through.

"We have a medic on the team," the rescue leader said. "We'll have him take a look at it. He'll take care of your arm too."

"My arm?" I looked down at my biceps and winced. There was a bleeding tear in the upper swell of my arm, right below the shoulder. Only once I acknowledged the wound did the tearing pain show up in its freezing/burning glory. Blood trickled past my elbow and dripped from my fingertips.

Another black-clad person—this one a female I instinctively knew shifted into some kind of feline—entered the room with two sets of medical scrubs. She passed one set each to Owen and me. She turned to the blue-eyed man to brief him on… something. She kept her voice low, and I needed information from Owen more than I needed to eavesdrop on their conversation. Besides, I didn't know who they were.

I leaned closer to Owen. "Who are these guys?"

"Shifter Council enforcers," Owen answered before the blue-eyed leader could.

"What are they doing here?" I asked him.

"David."

I blinked. "David?"

"When he called, he said he'd uncovered a tie between the family of Asiatic lion shifters in Iran and your doctor in Chicago. That's why he called. He wanted to warn us. He heard when the dudes in suits showed up. As I was being dragged away, he said something about contacting the enforcers." Owen explained all this while he tried to wriggle into the scrub pants using one hand.

I still held the blue fabric loose in my hand as I tried to process what he said. When I didn't say anything, he continued, "Well, his mom is on the Western regional council, so she's got contacts with all the different regional councils. The Great Lakes regional council is headquartered in Chicago."

"Right." I nodded. The explanation made sense, but I clearly had a lot to learn about shifter politics.

"Okay," the blue-eyed council enforcer said, turning back to us. "Let's get you checked out. We need to know what's been going on."

"My parents," I reminded him.

"Yes, I haven't forgotten. Two of my men will pick them up as soon as we have your address. We need to find out what they know about this whole mess."

Chapter Eighteen

THE enforcers' medic on duty did what he could for my injury. It helped that we were in a medical facility and the wound wasn't bad. What's a bullet graze compared to losing my parents or Owen? But there was no hiding the bandaging on my bicep.

Mom and Dad rushed into Dr. Mirza's waiting room looking as pale and haggard as I'd ever seen them, their council enforcer guards at their heels. They charged toward me, Mom barely stopping from launching herself at me. Her hand fluttered out as though to touch the bandage on my arm, but she stopped before making contact.

I stood from my chair and dragged her into a hug. She trembled in my arms and held on so tight I could barely breathe. She murmured what I knew to be words of love in Persian.

"I'm fine," I told her. "I promise."

Dad, after a quick glance assuring himself I seemed okay, became more concerned about the large number of big men with weapons stationed throughout the room. Benedict Snow—I'd finally found out the name of the commander of this little rescue mission—strode forward. "Mr. and Mrs. Franke, I've got some questions for you."

"You are not going to interrogate my parents," I snapped.

"They have information we need. Until today, we had no idea the Moreau Initiative had gotten as far as they have in their research."

"My parents don't know anything about that." Even knowing what Dr. Mirza said about the Frankes not being my biological parents, seeing them and their obvious concern for me, I *knew* they would never have knowingly allowed me to be a research subject. They'd been as duped by Dr. Mirza as I had been.

"The Moreau Initiative?" Owen asked, coming out from one of the back rooms where someone had found a sling for his arm. "Like *The Island of Dr. Moreau*? Nice to know they have a sense of humor."

Mom reached out to Owen, who looked a little taken aback. He took her offered hand, though. "You are hurt too? Why are my boys hurt?" she demanded of Snow.

"Your boys?" I asked her.

She scowled at me. "You are mine and he is yours, which makes him mine too."

She thought Owen was mine. Man, I wanted that to be true. And it was great, if a little weird still, to have Mom's wholehearted support. But I wasn't sure if I could claim Owen as mine. It wasn't safe to be around. Not yet.

The reminder of Paul and of what I'd done sobered me. I really wasn't safe to be around. Not for anyone. I stepped away from my mother.

"There's a conference room down the hall." Snow pointed.

I nodded, my parents following suit.

Dad rested his hand on my neck as we made our way across the lobby. I soaked up the touch. *Dad. My dad.* No matter what a paternity test might show, I believed it.

I stumbled to a stop at the doorway that opened into the hall. The same hall where I'd killed a man. My stomach lurched. My feet might as well have been cemented to the gray carpet. As much as I didn't need the reminder, I looked to the right. Paul's body was long since gone, but a blue tarp covered the floor. I could still smell his blood, though, and could make out some splatter along the walls.

A hand rubbed up along my spine, and I didn't have to turn to see it was Owen. A hundred people could touch me and I'd know instantly which one was him. "Focus," he whispered. He grabbed my hand and urged me to the left, the direction Snow and my parents had gone.

The conference room was kind of small, with a table that could seat ten people. I sat between my mom and Owen. Dad was on the other side of Mom. Snow and three of the council enforcers sat on the other side of us. One of the enforcers, the only female, dropped a pile of folders in front of Snow and took up a guard position at the door. Whether she was keeping people in or out was debatable.

Without preamble, Snow barked, "What is your connection to the Moreau Initiative?"

Everyone on my side of the table looked around. Finally, as though realizing the question had been directed to him, Dad said, "The what now?"

"The Moreau Initiative."

Dad shook his head. "It still doesn't mean anything to me."

"How long have you been aware of the existence of shifters?"

Snow's piercing blue glare took us all in, again making it hard to determine who he meant the question for.

"I have no idea what you're talking about," Dad said.

Mom shrugged in confusion.

"About a month," I said, trying not to see the startled expression on my parents' faces.

"My whole life," Owen said.

"What is a shifter?" Dad asked me.

"Ah...." I looked at Snow. He seemed to be the highest-ranking shifter representative in the room. It was his call.

He rolled his eyes. "They are human-animal shape-shifters. Individuals who can turn into animals." Snow's face was as bland as his voice, but his eyes watched my parents carefully.

Dad blinked.

Mom jerked back. "This is not the appropriate time for joking."

Snow leaned forward, resting his weight on his elbows. "So you are telling me you were unaware your son is a shifter."

"Joey?" Mom grabbed my hand, gaze raking over me.

I swallowed. Nodded.

Dad scowled at me, but I could see more concern than anger in his eyes. "That's not a nice trick to play on your mother."

"But she's not his mother, is she?" Snow asked.

Mom gasped, and her hold on my hands squeezed tight for a second.

"Hey." I glared at Snow. "She raised me and loved me and sacrificed for me. She is my mother and he is my father, no matter what the biology shows."

The color drained from Dad's face. Mom's eyes were wide with shock, pupils dilated.

"You—you know?" Mom's voice cracked.

"Not all of it," I said softly, adjusting our hands to weave our fingers together. "But I *am* a shifter, and, well, you and Dad aren't. Since it's inherited, there's no way we can be biologically related."

"But I am."

"Mom...." It wouldn't do any of us any good for her to continue lying about it.

Mom turned to my dad. "Joseph?"

Dad nodded. "It's time."

The council members leaned forward.

Under the table, Owen put his hand on my knee.

Mom said, "I am not your birth mother, but you are Farshid's—my brother's—son. I am you aunt."

"How? I mean, what happened? Who is my mother?"

Tears welled along the edge of her lids. A single drop hung for a second on the corner of her lashes before falling to slide down her cheek. "I did not meet your mother. My brother—your father—had gone to work at the wildlife preserve in—"

"The North Khorasan province," Owen broke in.

Mom lifted her gaze to him. "Yes. How did you know?"

"It would be the only place outside of India for your brother to have met an Asiatic lion shifter."

"Asiatic lion?" Dad asked.

"Uh, yeah. I turn into an Asiatic lion."

My parents examined me for a moment as though trying to see some leonine characteristics.

"What exactly is an *Asiatic* lion?" Dad asked.

At the impatient look we were getting from Snow and his cohorts, I decided the zoology lesson could wait. "Later."

We all focused on my mom. "Sometime before Joseph and I got married, Farshid called to tell me he'd met someone special. He was going to bring her to the wedding, but she did not come. A few months later, he called to tell me she was pregnant and he was to be a father. I was shocked, because there hadn't been a wedding, but I was his sister, not his mother, and he was happy."

She paused, eyes sad. "We didn't hear from him for several months. I... I was busy with my new husband and my new life. I didn't think much of it, even though we had been close. Then I got a letter telling me of the birth of his son, Ebrahim."

"Ebrahim?" I tried out the name my parents—my biological parents—had given me. It didn't feel quite right. After all this time, I was Yusuf. Joey to most, but Yusuf.

"We had to—" Mom began.

"Wait." Dad held up a hand, meeting each of the council enforcers' gazes before moving on. "Are you in any way connected with the US government? Or with any international government? I won't put my family at risk."

"We are not affiliated in any way with any nationally or internationally recognized government. We are part of the US Shifter Council, but we have no jurisdiction in nonshifter matters."

"Your word this does not leave the room?"

Snow nodded. The rest of the council enforcers did the same.

"Fine." Dad nodded for Mom to continue.

"A few months after the letter arrived, I got a call from Farshid. He said something was going on around the North Khorasan province. There was a facility there, and several of his wife's family—he called her wife, so I assume they were married at some point— had gone missing. Mostly children. He was worried about Ebrahim." Mom stopped to clear her throat.

Dad took over the story. "We made plans with Farshid. He and his family were going to come to us. We didn't hear from him for a couple of days. Our phone calls went unanswered. We didn't have his wife's name, or her family name, so I was going to go out there and see for myself. The day before I was to set out, a woman showed up at our apartment with a baby boy. With you." He looked at me.

"What happened?" My hands ached from the strong hold Mom had on me. I didn't mind, since my grip was equally as tight. Owen started rubbing his palm over my thigh in soothing circles.

"The woman, who claimed to be a cousin of your mother's, said there had been an attack, a robbery, so the officials would claim, and that your parents were killed."

A small sob escaped Mom's throat. This had to be horrible for her. Reliving her brother's death, on top of everything else today.

"She also said that while the official investigation stated robbery, it had been something else altogether. Your father had known they were coming and had sent you to Tehran, to us."

"He sent a letter, asking us to keep you, love you, and protect you. And to get out of Iran as soon as possible, because people—he thought a militia of some sort, but I'm guessing it was something related to you guys—" Dad indicated Snow and the gang. "—had taken over the territory and bribed government officials. They were looking for Ebrahim and would stop at nothing to get him.

"Legally getting custody of an Iranian child, especially when corrupt local officials claimed his mother's people wanted to take him in, was impossible. So instead I called in every favor I'd collected, spent all the money I had access to, changed your name, and got forged medical records showing you'd been born to Amaya and me. Then I went to the US Consulate and notified them of your birth and was issued your American birth certificate. A week later we were on a plane headed for the US."

"What was her name, my birth mother?" I asked.

Mom looked sad. "I do not know. My brother only ever called her his love and his wife."

I sucked in a breath to help me focus on the issues at hand. I faced Snow head-on. "Okay, now we've got that out of the way, you want to tell us how it ties in to our current situation?"

"Twenty-five years ago, the Moreau Initiative was very active in west Asia. The shifter groups there are solitary, and their isolation put them at risk. The Initiative began kidnapping and testing on those groups no one would miss. The International Shifter Consortium destroyed their base in the North Khorasan province fifteen years ago." He spoke matter-of-factly, but his eyes held regret. "The entire pride of Asiatic lion shifters there was destroyed."

I let out a pained gasp. The idea that I might have shifter family members—a pride—had been yanked away before it was fully formed. Stinging pressure built behind my eyes. I blinked back the urge to cry, telling myself I couldn't lose what I'd never had.

I cleared my throat and met Snow's gaze. "That's their story. And clearly they didn't know anything about Dr. Mirza and his freaky group."

"What does Dr. Mirza have to do with any of this?" Dad asked.

"Ah…." I looked at Snow, then at Owen. I really hoped they didn't expect me to explain.

Owen patted my thigh and spent the next ten minutes explaining what we'd found out about Dr. Mirza and his tests. He skipped over the incident with Paul. Snow and the enforcers didn't bring it up either. I appreciated their thoughtfulness more than I could say. The last thing I wanted was my parents to face the knowledge that their son had killed someone.

The pop of the rifle.

Owen slumping to the ground.

Rage.

Shifting.

Blood.

Watching them absorb the knowledge they had put me in the hands of a monster who wanted to run experiments on me instead of heal me… that was almost worse. Mom shook, wide-eyed and pale. She clutched at my arm, knuckles white. Dad, who up until now seemed to take the news mostly in stride, lost it.

He lurched to his feet, planting his fists on the conference table. "That son of a bitch! I'll kill him! Where is he? He told us… convinced us…." The anger drained from him, and he knelt between Mom and me. He cupped my cheeks and stared up at me.

"God, Joey. I swear to you. We didn't know. We only wanted what was best for you. And instead, we subjected you to a monster." Tears flowed freely from his eyes, and the guilt and the regret in them was more than I could take.

I pulled free of my mom's hold so I could place my hands over my dad's. "It's not your fault," I told him, pushing as much sincerity and belief into my words as I could. I needed him to hear me, to accept I meant what I said.

"If we hadn't trusted him—"

"Dad, don't. What other options did you have? I know you didn't set out to hurt me. *I know.* Would you have stopped looking for other doctors, other specialists? Let me die?"

"Of course not. But—"

"He'd have found me eventually. No doctor would have been able to diagnose me, not unless you somehow found a shifter doctor. And he was watching for a case like mine." I was trying to hold it together, I really was. But speaking rationally about this while my father was on his knees was more than I could do.

I slid off my chair and wrapped my arms around him. Mom joined us a second later. We cried for what we'd been through. We wept for what we'd lost.

Chapter Nineteen

MY parents wanted me to stay in Chicago. As much as I didn't want to add to the pain and drama of the weekend, I said no. I still needed to create my own life, my own future. As horrible as it was, the revelations had been cathartic. Painful, but cleansing. Maybe now we could heal as a family, get to know one another without the ghost of my illness hovering above us.

While I refused to consider leaving Cody College, I did agree to stay an extra few days before returning to campus. I couldn't afford more time than that—I had to be back in Wyoming before the next full moon. Eventually they relented.

The conversation with Owen the night before his flight back to Wyoming went a little differently.

"When I get back, I think it's best if we don't see each other anymore." I'd mentally rehearsed what I was going to say. I repeated the words over and over while in the shower. While brushing my teeth. While watching Owen pack his belongings into his duffel bag. We sat on my bed, him at the foot, me at the head, eyes locked.

Since we'd really never talked about whether we were officially together—one night fooling around did not make a relationship—it may not have been a breakup. But our time together certainly felt like more than friendship by this point. And, ultimately, it didn't matter. I wasn't safe to be around. Not yet.

"What do you mean?" His tone was even, calm. His scent, however, was anything but. There was a peppery hint of anger. The musty smell of hurt. My lion grew restless at the combination of smells and emotions. Owen was his/mine/ours to protect. And right there was the problem. In my head, the lion was a separate entity. And as long as I was unable to reconcile both sides of me— lion and man—I would constantly be battling myself for control. It would be like the autoimmune reactions I'd grown up with while my body tried to either reject or accept that part of my biology. But now the lion had manifested, and he was capable of hurting—of killing— someone. Emotionally, mentally, I was not prepared to deal with the reality of the predator inside me.

In the twenty-four hours since the events at Dr. Mirza's office, I'd lost count of the number of times Paul's death replayed in my head.

The pop of the rifle.
Owen slumping to the ground.
Rage.
Shifting.

Blood.

Insomnia was nothing new, but last night my dreams kept showing me dozens of scenes of flashing claws and jaws and blood. But instead of Paul, instead of someone who'd threatened me and someone I loved, I killed my mother. My father. Owen. Over and over, again and again.

When I didn't answer him right away, he asked, "It is the mother-hen thing? I know I tend try to take care of people, to act like I know best, when maybe they don't need it. I can try—"

Damn it. This was worse. I couldn't let him think it was anything he'd done. This was 100 percent about me and my issues. I had to try to explain. Owen deserved my honesty.

"Owen, I can't control myself when I shift. You and your dad both warned me, told me I needed to work with someone, but I didn't take it seriously. I thought I could just not shift. But, Owen, I *killed* someone. I didn't think, I reacted. What if I do that around you?"

"You won't."

"But I did. I *bit* you. You *bled.* And before, when I saw you and David together, I almost shifted. Even if I didn't hurt anyone, I could too easily accidentally shift in front of a human and put everyone at risk."

"What are you going to do? Become a hermit? Are you going to drop out of school? I fully support your decision to work on control. Of course I do. But you're being too hard on yourself. You've only been a shifter for a month. Not even a month, actually. You need to give yourself a break."

"A break? Owen, I *killed* somebody. There's no break from that."

He just watched me. Damn him and his compassionate eyes.

"The thing is, you eat at my control. Not your fault. But, Owen, I'm more than a little in love with you. My reactions around you are colored by that. They're more extreme, more volatile."

He sucked in a breath. "You… you love me?"

I ducked my head. Why had I said that? Well, because he deserved the truth. I nodded. "Yeah, I do. It would absolutely destroy me if I did anything to put you at risk."

"For how long?"

I jerked my head up. "What?"

"This distance you want to keep between us. How long do you plan to do it?" He didn't look worried or even compassionate anymore. The set of his jaw, the rounding of his shoulders… he was determined.

"I… I don't know. I have no idea how long something like learning to accept and/or control my inner lion might take."

Owen leaned forward, bringing our bodies a little closer together. I tried to ignore the warmth of his breath and the intensity of his gaze. "I'll give you three months."

"Three months," I repeated dumbly.

"Three months or whenever you feel your control is adequate for us to be together again. Whichever comes first."

"What happens in three months?"

"I come and get you. Because, Yusuf? I love you too, and I refuse to spend more than twelve weeks apart. So you take the time, work with Buddy or whoever to do what you need to do. I want you to be safe and happy, and if that means a *temporary* break, so be it. Make no mistake, it *is* temporary."

I almost missed most of what he said, too caught up in *I love you too*.

Dry-mouthed, I nodded. Three months. Or less. Suddenly I was very sure I'd be back before the deadline. I had some serious motivation.

Chapter Twenty

BUDDY the bear was a big believer in yoga.

Six weeks we'd been doing this. Six weeks. I didn't know how I expected him to teach me control, but hours upon hours of downward-facing dog and meditation wasn't it.

For someone who seemed to think inner reflection and relaxation techniques were so important, Buddy was the grumpiest person I'd ever spent time around. He was taciturn, ill-tempered, and generally seemed to prefer solitude to company. Despite his attitude and strange obsession with yoga, the big man's methods seemed to be working. I'd made it through my second full moon with Buddy last week, and the difference between it and the first one was enough to prove I was much more comfortable in my skin, so to speak.

When I'd shifted on purpose for the first time, it had been a slow and painful process. I'd been terrified I was going to do something horrible, and Buddy explained that those human emotions got in the way of a smooth transition. Once shifted, the cat took over almost completely. It was all instinct and primal drives.

Afterward, Buddy had me shifting twice a week. Once deep in the wilds of Buffalo Bill State Park, surrounded by nature. Once in my dorm room, surrounded by my human possessions. He said he was trying to get my subconscious to reconcile my shifted form with my human existence. Since he accompanied me on each shift, his regular appearance in my dorm room meant my neighbors probably thought I had standing hookup with an older man. But since Owen was the only person whose opinion on my love life mattered, I didn't particularly care if the guys down the hall gave me speculative looks.

When I'd shifted again at the full moon a couple of weeks ago, it felt right and natural, the animal consciousness there in the background, but my human side in charge. In the last couple of weeks, both halves started to coexist, to the point I didn't really view myself as having a human half or a shifter half. I was simply an individual, with aspects of both all the time.

I was halfway through Owen's deadline. He'd agreed to stay away for three months, and he'd been as good as his word. Sort of. I hadn't seen him in six weeks, which was a feat in and of itself, given we both lived at Matthison Hall. He didn't approach me, and I avoided the front lobby at night when I knew he'd be working. But he didn't leave me alone. I never saw him, but he was always there.

Every Monday, he sent me a text. It was always short, always simple—a heart icon, or a smiley face, or a simple "hi."

Every Tuesday I found a sticky note on my door when I left in the morning, something he'd clearly put there at the end of his shift at the front desk. Like the texts, these notes were simple, a few words to let me know he was thinking of me.

Every Wednesday he left a chess piece in my student mailbox.

Thursdays brought more texts, these with ridiculous internet memes attached.

I spent Friday evenings with Buddy, shifting or meditating in the woods. When I'd get back to my room, there was always a sandwich from the Union Center deli. It was never the same as a previous option and contained a combination of ingredients I would never have put together myself. Potato chips were always included.

Saturdays were the hardest. Whatever he left at my door was always something that had absorbed his scent. One week it was a soft and worn Cody College T-shirt, clearly not new, and it smelled so strongly of Owen it almost brought me to my knees. The next week it was a goofy stuffed owl he had to have slept with for his scent to be as ingrained as it was. I slept with the silly plush toy next to my head and his T-shirt under my pillow.

On Sundays, it was more sticky notes, these counting down the weeks.

It was obvious he didn't want me to forget about him. With or without the reminders, there was no chance of that happening. I knew there was no way I'd make it through six more weeks of this. My concentration was shot, and I was 99 percent sure I passed my classes on a fluke. We had a little over a week before the fall semester started, and since I didn't have lectures or exams to keep me occupied, my mind wandered to, and stuck on, Owen. Not that I needed the excuse. Every day I didn't interact with him, I felt it more, like the tugging in my chest when the moon was full. He was as much a part of me as my lion.

On Monday morning, I sent him a text. *Hi :)*

His response: *?! <3*

Tuesday was a bit more trouble. I realized I didn't know where Owen's room was. Deciding it was a good chance to practice my tracking skills, I went to the front desk to pick up his trail. My chest constricted at the first hit of his distinctive smell. My hands gripped the edge of the counter while I tried to breathe past the longing. When I'd gained control of my emotions, I found a recent line of Owen's nighttime-snow-and-fir scent. After a few false starts, I discovered that if I let some of the lion's instincts come forward, I could practically *see* Owen's trail. Which was actually pretty freaking cool.

I didn't have very far to go. Turned out, Owen's room was on the first floor, halfway down the north wing. When I reached his door, I could hear him shuffling around inside. The shuffling stopped, and I held my breath. I imagined he sensed me as clearly as I did him. I wanted to knock on his door, to see him face-to-face. To talk to him. To touch him. To just be in his presence for more than a moment or two.

Instead, I reached into my pocket and stuck the bright green sticky note to his door. I'd debated for hours, throwing away dozens of options before deciding on *Soon*.

I walked away before I gave in to temptation.

I skipped ahead in the pattern on Wednesday. Instead of the chess piece, I texted Owen a Grumpy Cat meme.

He texted back within seconds. *What are you up to, Yusuf?*

I hung a bag with an Italian sub with every possible topping from his door handle on Thursday.

I couldn't find a stuffed Asiatic lion anywhere, but I'd gotten my hands on a Care Bears Brave Heart Lion. I didn't know if Owen's sense of smell was anything like mine, but I made sure to handle the plush creature as much as possible before having it delivered to him at the front desk on Friday.

On Saturday, I slipped a postcard with a picture of the Chicago skyline into his mail slot.

It was three o'clock in the morning on Sunday, barely twelve hours after I'd given him the memento from Chicago, and nausea surged through me with every beat of my heart. I paused at the bottom of the steps, my palms damp with sweat. I tightened my grip on the heavy package I carried. I'd spent a near fortune on its contents, and, while not exactly fragile, I didn't want to see anything damaged.

Matthison Hall was mostly deserted. Most of the students who'd stayed over the summer were taking advantage of the short break before the fall semester to visit their families. I was glad for the emptiness, because I didn't want to deal with underage drunks or other insomniacs while I took this final step in my weeklong courting ritual.

I rounded the corner into lobby. Student mailboxes lined up on my right, and the poor plant that Owen had overwatered almost three months ago stood to my left. And just past the mailboxes was the counter.

Owen's wide amber eyes lasered in on me, his whole body stilling. The intensity of Owen's gaze had me biting my lip. The white-knuckled grip he had on his cell phone told me I wasn't the only anxious person in the room. It was ninety-seven steps from the entrance of the south wing to the entrance of the north wing. I only had to take thirty-six steps to reach Owen.

I had a whole speech prepared in my head. I silently rehearsed the words of gratitude and explanation as I took each of the thirty-six steps. Instead, the closer I got, the more words like *mine* and *never again* and *Owen Owen Owen* kept interrupting. Then, almost before I knew it, I stood in front of the counter. "Hey."

His throat convulsed as he gulped. He licked his lips. "Hey."

I set the present I'd ordered for him on the desk. The box was about eighteen inches long by eighteen inches wide, and about six inches tall. I'd wrapped it in pink paper with chubby unicorns frolicking across it. I'd seen it and knew Owen would probably get a kick out of the completely unsuitable wrap.

"This is for you," I said, in case the unicorns confused him.

His hand fluttered for a second, looking like he was reaching out to touch me rather than the package. A second later, he pulled back and started tugging at the taped flaps. Under the pink paper was a glossy wooden box with brass hinges and a little brass latch. The polished rosewood gleamed in the overhead lights. Owen traced his fingers across the top. He looked at me. "What is this?"

I squirmed. I'd never given anyone a present that meant so much to me. What if he hated it? What if he didn't understand its importance? What if he was tired of me?

The last I knew was insecurity talking, because his every note, his every gift over the last six weeks told me in no uncertain terms that he still wanted me.

"A present."

"I see that. But why?" His voice was steady, but I'd learned to trust all my senses. His snow-at-midnight scent was overlaid by nerves and hope, and his pulse pounded visibly at his neck.

"Just open it, okay?"

He released the brass latch, then lifted the lid to reveal chocolate brown and golden honey rosewood squares alternating across a hand-carved chessboard that had been made by an Iranian craftsman my mom knew. Owen's breath caught, his gaze finding mine. "Oh wow, Yusuf. This is beautiful." He reached into one of the two velvet bags that came with the board. Inside were the honey-colored, hand-carved chessmen.

I grabbed the other bag and withdrew one of the darker pieces. "Want to play?"

The smile that spread across his face was the one that had intoxicated me the first night—wide, rejuvenating, full of energy. It was sunshine after months of darkness. "Yeah, okay."

I set up the board while Owen brought one of the tall stools to the lobby side of the desk. He paused, eyes searching mine. He reached out as if to touch, then dropped his hand.

I didn't like the uncertainty in the action. Disliked even more the fact that I'd caused it.

I took his hand between mine and soaked up the contact. His fingers shook, but after a brief hesitation, he adjusted his grip until our fingers twined together. "Does this mean…." He stopped, inhaled deeply, then tried again. "What does this mean?"

"It means I want there to be a lot more late-night chess matches with you. I want there to be a lot more nights with you in general. I want… I want *you*." I stepped closer, well within his personal space bubble. Our chests nearly touched, and I had to tilt my head down a bit to be able to look him in the eye. I freed one hand and brought it up so I could trace his cheek. Then I brushed back his flyaway bangs before tracing his full lower lip with the edge of my thumb. His tongue darted out to tease my thumb, and all my blood rushed to my groin.

"No more ridiculous thoughts about keeping away from me for my own good?"

"First, they weren't idiotic thoughts, and second, I never actually said it was for your own good. But, no, I think I accomplished what I needed to."

"And you want to play chess with me?" His lips tipped with the slightest hint of a smile. He leaned in until our bodies actually touched, one of his arms looping around my back to hold me close.

"Among other things." My voice sounded deeper than usual. Rough.

"And you're not going to run away again?"

"I didn't—" I began, but at his arched brow, I changed what I was going to say. "No. No more running away. Besides, you didn't let me run far." I tugged at the hem of the T-shirt I wore. It was the one he'd given me, the one that smelled like him.

"Yeah, well, I understood why you had to do what you did. But you also needed to know you had somewhere—someone—to return to after your running was done."

I ducked my head, rubbing my cheek against his before turning to capture his lips with mine. It was gentle and sweet at first, but when Owen reached up to brace his hands on my shoulders and stand on his toes to deepen the kiss, I growled and opened my mouth for his questing tongue.

I wrapped my arms around his back, pulling him tight as though trying to merge our bodies. I pulled away to nibble along the corner of his mouth, to his jaw, back up behind his ear. "I love you," I murmured between kisses, over and over again.

"I'm totally in love with you too." He stroked along my spine, the contact soothing and arousing at the same time. If I were a common housecat, I'd probably be purring. As it was, it took all my concentration to keep from closing my eyes in bliss and basking in his touch.

"I didn't want to need anyone," I said ten minutes later. We'd slid to the ground, our backs against the front counter, and cuddled. We hadn't said much, too caught up in reacquainting ourselves with the feel of each other. "I was determined to make it or break it on my own."

"And then I came along with my own brand of mother-hen-style smothering." His head rested on my shoulder, his arm draped across my stomach.

"Good thing too. Turns out I do need something I can't take care of myself."

"Oh yeah? What's that?" He hugged me tight, and it was exactly what I needed.

"You. I need you, Owen Weyer."

Now Available

⟲REAMSPUN BEYOND

Stalking Buffalo Bill

By j. leigh bailey
A Shifter U Tale

A smitten coyote isn't the only one stalking Buffalo Bill.

A buffalo walks into a cafe. Sounds like the start of a bad joke, but for coyote shifter Donnie Granger, it's the beginning of an obsession. Donnie is a little hyperactive and a lot distractible, except when it comes to William. He finally works up the nerve to approach William but is interrupted by a couple of violent humans.

While William—*don't call me Bill*—is currently a professor, he once worked undercover against an international weapons-trafficking ring. Before he can settle into obscurity, he must find out who leaked his location and eliminate the thugs. He tries keeping his distance to protect Donnie, but the wily coyote won't stay away.

It'll take both Donnie's skills as a stalker—er, hunter—and William's super-spy expertise to neutralize the threat so they can discover if an excitable coyote and a placid-until-pissed buffalo have a future together.

Now Available

⊙REAMSPUN BEYOND

Chasing Thunderbird

By j. leigh bailey
A Shifter U Tale

A legendary love.

Ornithology professor Simon Coleman's reputation
is at risk, and the only way to save his name is to
prove thunderbirds are more than creatures of Native
American myth. Grad student and part-time barista
Ford Whitney has a lot on his plate, but it's also his duty
to make sure the resident bird nerd doesn't discover
shape-shifters—like himself—live on campus.

When a series of incidents related to Simon's
search put him in harm's way, Ford's instincts kick
in, and they become closer than is strictly proper for
student and teacher. Ford is forced to reveal his secrets
to Simon, and their relationship is put to the test—
Simon must choose between salvaging his reputation
and protecting the man who protected him....

Coming in August 2018

◯REAMSPUN BEYOND

Dreamspun Beyond #25
Star-Crossed Lover by Liv Olteano

A love worth crossing the stars for.

Taka has been a dreamcatcher and part of Team 32 for over six decades, but nobody has tempted him like Ginger—a dancer at club Zee. Too bad dreamcatchers aren't allowed to have meaningful relationships with regular people. His willpower proves a finite resource, though, when a mission at the club means spending much more time around Ginger.

Ginger's infatuation with Taka is unwavering. When he proves to have some paranormal skills of his own, he earns himself a place on the team—if he wants it. His decision will change his life—not to mention Taka's—irrevocably.

But living in the now could prove an issue for a man who has as much history as Taka. Can Ginger's determination help him make his way into Taka's heart?

Dreamspun Beyond #26
Hex and Candy by Ashlyn Kane

True love's kiss can break the curse. But then what?

Cole Alpin runs a small-town candystore. He visits his grandmother twice a week. And sometimes he breaks curses.

Leo Ericson's curse is obvious right away, spiderwebbing across his very nice body. Though something about it worries Cole, he agrees to help—with little idea of what he's getting into.

Leo is a serial monogamist, but his vampire ex has taken dating off the table with his nasty spell, and Leo needs Cole's companionship as much as his help. When the hex proves to be only the beginning of his problems, Leo seeks refuge at Cole's place. Too bad magic prevents him from finding refuge in Cole's arms.

Cole's never had a boyfriend, so how can he recognize true love? And there's still the matter of the one responsible for their troubles in the first place....